Rave Reviews for JAKE A

Jake and the Tiger Flight is more than an exciting story about discovering the magic of airplanes and the heroism of those who fly them. It provides readers of all ages with practical ways to turn their dreams into reality. And guess what? The book actually makes it fun to learn the meaning of responsibility, self-discipline, and goal-setting.

—Barry Schiff, retired airline captain (TWA), record-setting pilot, and award-winning aviation author

Jake and the Tiger Flight made me wish I was a kid again. This book is a gem for middle school students and adults alike—adventure, drama, excitement, and character development all rolled into one easy-to-teach package. A must for any middle grades reading curriculum.

—Joe McKenzie, retired Army officer and middle grades teacher for 12 years

What a great idea: an enjoyable read for pre- and young teens with a real point and an incentive to actually "stick with it." Something to encourage getting away from both TV and computer screens. I'd think parents would love it. I know I have.

—Gregg Loomis, pilot and author of *The Sinai Secret*

Learning to fly is an unforgettable experience, and one that is likely to leave you fascinated with aircraft and the world of flight for a lifetime. This book should encourage many fledglings to stretch their wings.

—A. Hugh Adams, President Emeritus, Broward Community College, Fort Lauderdale, Florida

I really loved this book! I read it cover to cover without putting it down. It's cute, well written and has a great message. Tying aviation to a message about living responsibly is clever and insightful and worth reading.

—Patty Wagstaff, National Aerobatic Champion and Air Show Pilot

Jake and the Tiger Flight reveals to young readers how dreams and ambitions are ultimately realized through hard work and in being a responsible person. It's an inspiring read filled with life lessons for students and for their parents.

—Michael Buchanan and Diane Lang, authors of *Micah's Child* and award-winning teachers

I enjoyed *Jake and the Tiger Flight* very much. It brought out the excitement and adventure all boys and girls want to experience with aircraft! The book will inspire boys and girls—and maybe adults as well—to go after their dreams and make them come true. It really is a neat, suspenseful book!

—Pat Epps, award-winning pilot, explorer, aviation business promoter and entrepreneur

WOW! WHAT A BOOK! I could not put it down! My kids will love it at school! I just need to know when the 2nd book will be out! It was wonderful. I know just how Jake felt.

—Barbara White, elementary grades teacher for 23 years

by
George Weinstein

with
Marty Aftewicz

Story by
Phil "Sunny" Cataldo

TIGER FLIGHT PRESS

Jake and the Tiger Flight is a work of fiction. Though some names and places are real, they are used fictitiously. The work as a whole is a product of the author's imagination.

TIGER FLIGHT PRESS

ISBN-13: 978-0-9817149-0-5
ISBN-10: 0-9817149-0-0

www.tigerflightfoundation.org

For information:
Tiger Flight Press
1285 Willeo Creek Drive
Roswell, GA 30075.

Printed in the United States of America

COVER ILLUSTRATION BASED ON PHOTOGRAPHY BY MARY KENNEDY

COVER & TEXT DESIGN BY PAMELA TRUSH OF DELANEY-DESIGNS

Proceeds from sales of this book benefit the 501(c)(3) nonprofit Tiger Flight Foundation and its mission to lead the young to fulfill their dreams, including the dream of flight.

Acknowledgments

The author and contributors owe a significant debt to
our manuscript readers and consultants:

David Wright
Tom Calvanelli
Bill Jansson
Keith Walker
Clint Johnson
Bart Barber
Neil Gatewood
Susan Cataldo
Michael Buchanan
Mark All
Kathleen Boehmig
Sid Versaci
John Witkowski
Brooks Dumas
Tom Leidy
John Sheffield
June Smith
Marre Stevens
Adam Patton
Debora Ondracek and her 5th grade class at Porterdale Elementary School:
Amy, Ann-Marie, Antonia, Blake, Briana, Cameron, Cristen, Jade,
Jeremy, Joshua, Keiera, Kinsee, Kureece, Lemoine, Venessa, and Zach

Robin Berlin and her 6th grade reading class at
Taylor Road Middle School: Asa, Chase, and Neal

And thanks especially to Katherine Weinstein, who makes everything "jake"

CHAPTER ONE

Jake Skyler hunched over his newest portable video game, "Perils of Perinox," the bright yellow console smooth and slick in his hands. He looked through the eyes of a tough, battle-tested Space Marine. At the bottom of the screen, the barrel of the Marine's deadly laser gun swung one way and then the other, following Jake's thumb taps.

He had moved the Marine across a misty swamp, shooting up a bunch of the squid-like Perinoxians along the way, and made it into the maze of dungeons where the monsters' leader was hiding. Inching the Marine forward, Jake tried to anticipate the next attack. Around the corner, just ahead? From one of the holes in the low stone ceiling? Maybe even up through those wide grates in the floor. All he could hear was the drip, drip, drip from the squidies' wet lair.

Jake eased the Space Marine toward the corner, blaster ready, and—

"Jake!"

His twelve-year-old body jerked so hard that the handheld

leaped from his fingers and turned a somersault in the air. Jake caught it in time to see two squidies reach up through the floor grates and pull him to his screaming doom. They laughed in a liquid gurgle as they did it.

Jake switched off the device, rocked back in his padded deck chair beside the backyard patio table, and said, "Thanks, Mom, you got me killed."

"What's going to get you killed is not paying attention. I called you twice already." His mother, still dressed in her business clothes, stood as tall and regal as an imperial queen, ruler of ten galaxies, master of a thousand alien races, judge and jury of Jake. Her eyes were haunted, as if she'd seen things too terrible to mention while sitting on her throne.

From the look on Mom's face, Jake knew he was more trouble than ruling ten whole galaxies and all those alien races put together. She stood close by. He was so into the game he'd missed hearing her come out through the sliding-glass door and walk across the deck.

Mom said, "I can see you wandering into the street playing that stupid game." In one hand, she held something rolled up. It was either a stun-probe from the ninth moon of Yurt or the letter his teacher made him bring home from school.

"I always look both ways before crossing the street," he said, shifting the handheld from his left hand to his right so he could wipe each palm on his jeans. They were suddenly sweaty.

"You always have your nose down in that game or you're staring up at the clouds." She shook the tube of paper at him. "Daydreaming," Mom said. "That's what your math teacher wrote in this letter. You're always daydreaming in class."

He opened his mouth to defend himself—he wasn't *always* daydreaming in class, he was sure to pay attention when Mrs. K and the other sixth grade teachers talked about cool stuff—but his mom said, "According to Mrs. Kirby, you don't pay attention. You forget to do things that she asks, and you don't finish your assignments. Right now, on the kitchen table, there's your math homework with twenty problems but you left the last six undone."

Jake lowered his head. Busted.

He'd read Mrs. K's letter on the bus, of course. Read it three times, feeling more and more ashamed, and even considered forging his parents' signatures but Mrs. K had a reputation for following up with a phone call on notes sent home. He wasn't a bad kid, but somehow he couldn't stay on target, couldn't get things done. Even now, with Mom looking so upset, he wanted to hunker down and have another go at those tricky Perinoxians.

But no. He had to sit there and listen. As he looked up at the imperial queen, he saw far behind her head a cloud that looked like the coolest spaceship. His gaze drifted to that sleek shape bristling with a hundred laser cannons—

"Jake, are you even listening?"

"Yeah, I was—"

She hollered, "Why am I wasting my breath on you?"

The sliding-glass door whisked aside and Dad marched out into the sunlight, ready to double-team him. Jake's rugged, wide-shouldered father wore work clothes: a denim shirt and khakis smudged with some kind of grime, probably from moving stuff at his hardware store. However, Jake pretended it was blood and that Dad was the imperial queen's royal executioner. His strength and angry frown fit the role.

Dad stabbed his thick finger at the handheld still in Jake's grip and said, "Put that down. Your mother told me about that letter you brought home."

Mom said, "We were just talking about it. At least I was talking about it—Jake's staring at some clouds."

Jake dropped the game console on the patio table with a loud clunk. He hated it when they ganged up on him. Staring at his empty hands, he waited for The Big Lecture.

Dad paced across the deck, saying, "It's our fault, I guess. We've been too easy on you."

"Speak for yourself, Nick." Mom said, and Jake silently agreed with her. His father usually let him off the hook; it was the imperial queen who always punished him.

As Jake thought about that, Dad snapped his fingers in front of Jake's face. Thanks to being zinged by Mom, Dad was now even angrier. He said, "Pay attention. Learning to focus, to follow through on your assignments, to listen when people are talking to you, these are the kinds of things that show you're growing up." He started to pace again, hands clenched into fists. "'Finish what you start.' That's what my father—your grandpa—said to me when I was your age. It applies to homework and everything else you do."

Mom said, "Jake, it's time you become more responsible. Your father and I decided you need some structure outside of school—something to focus your mind."

Dad jumped in again. "We want you to spend your Saturdays working at the hardware store with me." He looked hard at Jake—this wasn't a question or an offer to consider. It was a "Do it or else" situation.

Jake hated the idea, but decided their punishment could've been worse. Much worse. Losing his Saturdays meant missing some good shows, but he could record those and watch them later. The bad part was that his video game skills would get rusty—it was something you had to do all the time if you wanted to stay sharp. When his buddies from school came over every Sunday for a whole afternoon of eating pizza, surfing the Net, and gaming, he wouldn't do as well as he usually did. Maybe he could practice a little at the store when Dad wasn't looking.

At least his father had left his Sundays free. He'd die if he had to work all weekend—and his buddies would never forgive him if they lost their favorite place to crash.

He grumped, "I guess learning about tools and stuff would be okay."

Mom nodded with approval, but the look on her face said, "*Better not mess up, kiddo.*"

CHAPTER TWO

Dad's pickup truck rode way off the ground. Jake loved feeling as tall as a giant, looking down into the cars they passed.

His dad's hardware store—with the big red-and-white checkerboards on either side of "Skyler Hardware, Sky-High Service at Rock-Bottom Prices"—sat along the highway on the outskirts of Rome, Georgia. In the distance was Lavender Mountain, with miles of spring-green fields and piney woods leading up to it, the tallest peak in Floyd County.

Dad backed into a parking space far from the front door, leaving the best spots for his customers. He spread his hands and said in a funny, melodramatic voice, "Someday, son, all of this will be yours."

Jake peered out the windshield at the large, barn-like store his grandfather had built fifty years ago. Heavy equipment for rent was lined up on one exterior wall near concrete and iron figurines for people's yards. Shelves of springtime flowers flanked the door. In the back, wood pallets had been stacked up beside the dumpster. It was definitely part of the family history and he liked to drive the mini tractors and stuff, but he said, "Wow, Dad, I don't know."

His father shrugged. "It was always my dream to run my own business, but that doesn't have to be your dream." He pointed at Jake. "What do you dream about doing one day?"

"If I practice hard enough, I can be the best video gamer in the—"

"I mean a big, important dream. What do you want to do with your life?"

Besides racking up the high score on every game invented? Hmmm…

Jake opened the door and climbed out of the truck. When his dad bought it a couple of years before, Jake had dreaded the long drop to the ground, but now the step down didn't seem so bad. He'd gotten taller, five-foot-three the last time he checked. He was growing up. What did he really want to do when he was all grown up anyway?

He had no idea.

Everything he liked to do was make-believe. As a grownup, he probably couldn't pretend all day, because lately grownups were always reminding him, "You can't spend your life with your head in the clouds."

"Jake?" Dad was staring at him. "Are you going to close the truck door and come in, or should I hang a sales tag around your neck and sell you as a lawn ornament?"

"Sorry, Dad. I was just thinking about your question." He shut the door, embarrassed to be caught "wool-gathering" again, as his Grandma Skyler called it. Patting his jeans pocket to make sure the handheld game was there, he followed his father into the store.

Dad turned off the security system and switched on the lights. He'd updated the rows of shelves, pegboards, and other displays, but the original creaky, wide-plank wood floors were still there. He asked, "So, what's the big, important dream you settled on?"

"I really don't have a clue."

Dad laughed through his nose. "That's okay. If you're lucky, someday soon you'll know. And you can get fired up about one dream today and another one tomorrow. It'll be something you're already doing or it'll sneak up on you unexpectedly, coming from out of the blue."

"What'll it feel like when I know?" Jake asked, frustrated that he couldn't quite picture this dream thing. Not having one made him worried—it was as if he'd been daydreaming when the real dreams were being handed out and he missed his turn.

"You'll be as sure of your dream as you are of your own name." Dad flipped over the sign on the door, declaring that his store was open for business. "When my father used to bring me here to help out on weekends, one day I just *knew* this is where

I could spend my life—running my own business, calling the shots, answering to no one. It hit me like a thunderbolt." His smile widened. "Hey, maybe you'll learn to love it too."

Jake forced a smile for his dad. He said, "Yeah, maybe so."

The morning dragged by as he tried to stay focused on counting everything in the store. He would match his number with what the computer said was supposed to be there, and write down any corrections beside the endless columns of figures on a thick printout. Whenever he grew bored and began to explore the long aisles of the store, his father ordered him back to work. After a few hours, Jake was sure of one thing: counting hardware was *definitely* not what he wanted to do with his life.

Around noon, with the handheld feeling heavy in his pocket and the Perinoxians whispering squidy taunts in his ears, he asked his dad if he could take a break and go outside.

"Yeah, sure thing, bud," Dad said in a tough-guy voice. "Going out back for a smoke?" Jake gave him a dirty look and Dad put up his hands. "Just kidding. Sheesh, what a grouch."

Jake closed the back door before he took out the handheld. It felt wrong to be playing instead of working, like he was doing something as bad as smoking a cigarette. Dad never took a break and he'd been going nonstop since they got there, helping customers, unpacking boxes, answering the phone, and paying bills. All the while he smiled, happy to be where he was and doing whatever needed doing, in love with his work, his “dream.”

Hopefully when his own dream came knocking, Jake thought, it would make him feel like that. Sitting on the back stoop, he switched on the handheld and selected “Perils of Perinox” from the menu. His guilt evaporated as he lost himself in the awesome graphics and sound effects. His reflexes were sharp, his aim better than ever as the Space Marine crossed the misty swamp, shooting slimy monsters to pieces. Maybe by the time he grew up there would be a starship academy and he could go around the universe hunting down evil creatures. Talk about a dream. Bzzzp, bzzzp—take that, squidy!

His Space Marine advanced quickly to the dungeon corridor where Mom had interrupted the battle and gotten him killed. This time he knew to watch the floor grates for tentacles.

A new sound wormed its way into his thoughts, the rumbling drone of an engine. The deep, powerful thrum didn’t sound like a car or truck. Maybe an airplane? He knew there was an airport across the highway, but the noise was so near—the only planes he’d seen were way up high. As it grew louder, he realized that he heard more than one engine, more like three or four. He could barely concentrate on the game.

The throaty rumble now filled his ears. It vibrated in his chest and rattled his bones. The sound became a part of him. Instead of being scared, he liked the feeling.

No, he loved it.

Surrendering to these new sensations, Jake looked up from the game. Time ebbed and everything moved in slow motion. Slow enough that he could see and memorize every detail.

Four airplanes rushed toward him, not much higher than the roof of the store. He'd never seen planes like these. Their bellies were creamy white, and the rest of each aircraft was painted bright orange, with wavy black tiger stripes. Instead of having just one tail, each plane had two fins that jutted out from the sides, forming a wide letter H. Twin-tailed tigers!

They flew in a tight diamond formation, their wingtips only a few feet apart, with one in the lead, one on each side, and one trailing. The airplanes were so close to him he could even see the pilots, who all wore black baseball caps and sunglasses. As Jake stared up, the lead pilot looked down at him and saluted. It was like a movie hero reaching out of the screen to pull Jake into a fantasy world and make him magical too. He saw me, Jake thought. *He* saw *me*!

A chill raced over his arms and down his back. It went even deeper than where the engines vibrated his bones, to a place in his soul where it slid in as smooth as a key, then turned like a stunt plane doing a rollover, unlocking something inside.

He'd never thought of flying planes as something he wanted to do. Now, however, he could imagine piloting in the lead tiger aircraft, looking down on a kid while he kept his formation tight. He really could envision himself up there in the cockpit and it felt *right*. Was this what Dad had been talking about?

The whole show seemed to be just for him. It was a dream served up on a tiger-striped platter. He hadn't missed out after all!

His body, a tightly bound spring, suddenly uncoiled. He jumped up and down and waved his arms at the pilots. The Perinoxians were long forgotten. "Hey!" he shouted. "Hey!"

He felt as light as the air under those amazing wings. "Heyyyyyyyyyyyyyy!"

Then time sped up again. The formation zoomed past him and over the roof of the hardware store. They slid smoothly from a diamond shape into a tight diagonal line, an orange and black arrow slicing through the sky.

Jake raced around the corner of the building to keep them in sight. Each aircraft turned sharply above the highway, following the plane in front of it—one, two, three, four. He wanted to chase them across the road and follow them forever, but they disappeared from view beyond the trees. The twin-tailed tigers were descending rapidly, no doubt heading for the airport.

Fighting for breath in the parking lot, Jake still enjoyed the rumble of the engines in his chest, as deep as a tiger's growl. The colors around him—the sky and grass and cars going by—were more intense than he'd ever seen.

This is it, he said to himself. This is what a dream feels like.

Closing his eyes, he replayed the flight of the four tigers again and again. He saw the pilot's salute, the man looking right at him. Such a gift should've been enough, but he knew he wouldn't be happy until he saw those planes up close. Until he sat in the cockpit. Until he flew.

CHAPTER THREE

At supersonic speed Jake ran into the store through the front door and roared up to his father, who was helping a man select a power drill. Gasping, Jake couldn't figure out what to say first.

Dad asked, "Are you okay?" Jake gulped and nodded as his father said, "Well, don't interrupt. Go back to your work and I'll be over as soon as I can." He turned his back to Jake and resumed his description of some kind of drilling technique.

The dismissal hurt Jake's feelings, but replaying the scene with the airplanes filled him with excitement again. He had to get a closer look at those twin-tailed tigers immediately.

His creative mind plotted and planned, finally settling on a strategy: convince his dad to let him get off work early and then go explore the airport. Dad had repaired an old bike of Jake's, which still was in the back of the store because Jake had received a new one for Christmas. With the house only a mile away down the highway, practically a straight shot, he was sure his father would let him ride the bike there. Even if he took a small detour past the airfield, he'd get home before Dad, so he wouldn't "arouse suspicion," as they say on TV.

After ringing up the sale and wishing the customer well, his father strolled toward Jake, who got busy counting hammers. Dad said, "I didn't know that game console had a calculator in it."

"Huh?" Jake frowned and then followed his father's gaze to the handheld, which sat on the floor where he'd dropped it beside the printout. He'd forgotten all about it.

Dad said, "Do whatever you want on your break, but when you're on the job, you're supposed to be working. Got it?"

Jake felt his face redden with embarrassment. "Got it," he said.

"Good." Dad picked up the device and pushed it into Jake's jeans pocket. "Now what did you come in all excited about?"

"Uh, no big deal, just something I saw."

Dad said, "I heard some planes go overhead. Did they surprise you?"

Play it cool, Jake told himself. "Yeah, I guess. Could I leave work around 3:00 maybe?"

His father looped his thumbs in his belt and said, "Quitting time is 6 o'clock."

"I know, but it's my first day and—"

"A responsible person doesn't quit his job in the middle of things to go have fun. He sticks to it. Remember: finish what you start."

Dad's tone told Jake that the discussion was over. In his mind, the sound of the airplane engines grew fainter as they flew away. Then he couldn't hear them at all.

"Yes, sir," he muttered and went back to counting the stupid hammers.

By 4:00, he was dragging his feet from pegboard to shelf, having to start over on many of his counts because his thoughts drifted back again and again to the tiger-striped planes. Somehow, even the best video game in the world, with the toughest monsters and deadliest weapons, couldn't match their real-life magic. And the lead pilot saluting him was the best part. He felt like King Arthur after Merlin tapped the sword Excalibur on his shoulders. Except after that happened to Arthur, he didn't go back to mucking out stables—he became King of Camelot—while here Jake was counting toilet plungers. Woo-hoo.

Dad peered over the cash register as Jake shuffled past and said, "Are you deflating?"

"What?"

"I keep hearing this sighing sound—'hmmmmmm'—and thought maybe you'd sprung a leak. And you're wearing the longest, gloomiest expression I've seen since we lost our Internet connection for a whole day."

Jake said, "I'm fine."

"Yeah right. You forgot to add, 'Hmmmmmm.'" His dad rapped his fingertips on the cash register. "Well, I can't have my customers come in and see Jake the Zombie Boy slouching around. It's bad for business." With a glance at his watch, he said, "I finally repaired that old bike of yours. Think you could ride it home without getting into trouble?"

Jake wanted to leap in the air and pump his fist at this turn of luck, but he knew he needed to stay low-key. If he'd been trying to act pitiful, he probably would've blown it. Actually being pitiful saved the day! He said, "Yes, sir. I have a key, in case Mom isn't there."

"Go on then, before you sigh all the air out of your body."

Careful to remain casual, Jake took slow steps to the back of the store and retrieved the old bike and his scuffed-up helmet with a new chinstrap, courtesy of Dad. He ambled along the aisle to the front, where he placed the printout beside the cash register. Not wanting to act overeager to escape, he said, "If you want, I can come in tomorrow and work on it some more."

His father blinked at him and Jake hoped he hadn't overplayed it. Smiling, Dad said, "No, that's okay. I'll put these changes in the computer and have a new list for you next Saturday. Thanks for your help, partner. Be careful on your way home."

Jake promised he would be and eased out the front door, rolling his bike alongside him. After strapping on his helmet, he sped down the wide shoulder of the road. Every dip or bump made his knees smack the handlebars because he'd gotten too big for the bike. At least he still could stand up on the pedals and make it go really fast, almost like flying. He was free!

At a traffic light, he waited for a green in his favor and crossed the highway. He reached the Richard B. Russell Regional Airport in a few minutes, but then faced another setback. A tall chain-link fence protected the entire property. Barbed wire topped the fence for as far as he could see in either direction. Beyond, a half dozen small aircraft sat idle. None was painted orange with black stripes, but those tiger planes had to be there somewhere. How to get inside?

The first gate he came to could only be opened by entering a code into a payphone-like keypad. Panting a little from his bike ride, Jake wiped his sweaty forehead as he followed the fencing. It stopped at the long, pale yellow metal wall of an airplane hangar and then started up again at the opposite corner of the building. The fence went on to border a parking lot with a dozen cars. A one-story brick and glass building at the end of the lot served as "Fixed Based Operations" for the airport, according to a sign. But he couldn't wander in there and look for a way onto the airfield—people would notice a kid snooping around.

On the other side of the chain link was a huge old plane, its top half in white and lower half in olive drab. In bright yellow, someone had painted "Tiger Lady" on its nose, below the cockpit windows. It didn't look like a tiger, but maybe it was a clue that he was closing in on the twin-tailed aircraft. Jake decided his best bet to find them was the hangar that bisected the fence. They would need a big place to put those four planes. Large windows ran along the side of the building, but they were too high up to see through, even when he stood on his bike pedals. No help there. He knew there was only one way to find out for sure: get inside the hangar.

Taking his time to peer more closely at the fence beside the parking lot, he spotted a narrow gate he'd overlooked before. It was labeled "Pedestrian Entrance." A way onto the airfield! This was more exciting than finding a secret passage in a video game.

If someone was in the hangar, he'd ask if he could have a quick look, to see if the planes were there. He rehearsed what he would say. Leaving his bike against the pale yellow wall, he eased toward the edge of the building. He peeked around the corner in time to see a tall, mustached man wearing an tan-colored flight suit and a black ball cap slide the metal hangar doors together. They closed with a grating rumble.

The man strode to a pickup truck parked on the opposite corner from Jake, climbed in, and drove around the other side of the building. Seconds later, behind Jake, the electronically controlled gate began to open—the man driving the truck was sure to spot him. Maybe the guy would grab him for trespassing and hold him down until the police arrived.

Jake dashed along the fence to the pedestrian gate, pushed it open, and raced to the front of the hangar where he'd be hidden from the driver. Hopefully the man wouldn't notice the bike in the deep shadow below the windows. The rumble of the truck faded as the man drove away.

With a sigh of relief, Jake scanned the hangar entrance. To the left of the sliding doors, a giant banner mounted on the building showed a blue shield edged with yellow, like something the Knights of the Round Table would've carried, on which was painted a winged tiger with two tails and a lightning bolt streaking beneath its belly. Below the picture were the words "Tiger Flight."

Awesome.

Sneaking inside wasn't such a good idea, but he hated to chicken out at the last minute. Also, he felt exposed to anybody crossing the airfield or glancing out the Fixed Based Operations windows. Before he could argue himself out of his decision, Jake yanked a handle on one side of the double doors. The rollers squeaked so much he knew security people would come running, but no one appeared. He'd moved the door only a few feet, but it was wide enough to change his life.

Skylights in the high, slanted ceiling let in long cones of late-afternoon sunshine. Jake caught his breath. The sunlight illuminated rich orange and velvet black. The aerial tigers crouched in a half circle, facing him, as if waiting for his command. It was like finding the hiding place of UFOs, the riches of the pharaohs, and the secrets of Atlantis all rolled up in one.

Blood pounded in his ears, and he trembled with excitement as he slipped inside the hangar. Sunlight glinted on the closed cockpits, caused the white undersides to glow with reflected light, and emphasized the fascinating H-shaped tails. It made the orange paint blaze across the wings and along each fuselage. The black stripes seemed to wave, like the skin of a tiger rippling when it flexed its muscles.

Jake remembered the open door behind him and reluctantly turned to close it. He didn't want to look away from the planes for even a second. With the doors pushed tight together again, he whirled, afraid that this had been a dream or a mirage or just another of his fantasies.

The four tigers still faced him. They seemed to call his name. *Jake, come closer. Touch our skins. We'll take you everywhere you want to go.*

Feeling like the big-cat trainer at the circus, he sensed their power as he stepped into the semi-circle of orange and black and white. More details emerged as he crept closer: the yellow spiral painted on each propeller nose cone, the small lights mounted in the low-slung wings, the Tiger Flight shield on the outside of each tail fin along with letters and numbers. The engines, which were located behind the propellers, gave off the hot-metal odor of machines that recently had worked hard. Jake touched the tiger-painted metal that covered one engine—warm under his hand. Other than his breathing, Jake heard no sounds.

The first plane he examined bore the designation N5695F below the shield. At that moment, he couldn't remember his own name, but N5695F was burned in his brain.

He walked around each plane once and then traveled in figure-8s as he looped between the aircraft. His fingers grazed the smooth metal skins until he knew them like he knew his own face. He memorized each plane's letter-number combination on the H-tails and even the tread design on the three wheels. Nothing escaped his eyes and hands.

After a final tour around the planes, Jake realized he desperately wanted to sit in one of the cockpits. He returned to N5695F and tried to decide the easiest way to get inside.

On the wing, near the body of the plane, a black box with yellow lettering warned "NO PUSH" but didn't say anything about no standing or stepping. Jake took a running jump and landed there. Surprisingly, the metal flexed under his sneakers. He'd figured that the planes were made of steel, practically bulletproof.

He studied the closed cockpit with its curved, three-piece design. His fingers fit perfectly in the seam where the orange frame met the clear Plexiglas. He tugged along the canopy, delighted when the middle third of the cover slid back.

With a short step, he cleared the edge of the cockpit and stood on the pilot's seat. He plopped down on the cushioned, light gray leather and gaped at all of the dials and controls crammed into such a small space. Even more amazing, nothing was labeled; the Tiger Flight guys needed to remember what each one meant.

His feet kicked in midair since his legs weren't long enough to reach the two silver-colored pedals he saw on the floor. Brake and accelerator? So many mysteries. He gripped a rubber-coated steering wheel that only had sides on it—no top or bottom arch. The whole steering column moved when he pushed it forward and pulled it back toward him, like a videogame joystick. To his right, identical controls, steering, and pedals were duplicated for the seat beside him. Behind the seats, a small, carpeted space bore a yellow-lettered sign that read, "BAGGAGE AREA 75 LBS MAX." He could get a dog and fly him all over the world!

As soon as he thought this, he remembered that feeling of something unlocking inside of him, the confidence that he could do anything. Fly all over the world? Maybe that's what he wanted to do when he grew up. It sure was what he wanted to do right then and there.

He pretended to push some of the buttons on the console and made the sound of a powerful engine coming to life. In his mind, the propeller turned slowly and then sped up so fast it became a blur. The hangar doors magically parted as he accelerated forward, and he zoomed outside and then along the runway and up, up, up into the beautiful spring sky.

Turning the wheel left and right, he swept past clouds that looked like spaceships and castles and the dog he wanted. He set his sights on the likeness of a Perinoxian and blasted it with the machine guns that had emerged from the wing's headlights. Gotcha, squidy!

He celebrated with aerobatic stunts: figure-8s, loop-de-loops, barrel rolls, and power dives. The wind screamed past as he shot through the sky. Ahead, another monster loomed and he armed the missiles that appeared under his wings.

Just as he prepared to fire, a metallic sound reverberated from the closed hangar doors. Clank-clank-clank-clank-clank and on and on, like a chain being pulled through the door handles on the outside. Then the snap of a lock.

Crap! His daydream evaporated like water on a piping hot stove. He was trapped!

CHAPTER FOUR

The air inside the hangar felt still and thick. Jake hopped out of the cockpit, shoes thumping onto the wing, and jumped to the concrete floor. Though it was only a few feet, it jarred him like the long drop from Dad's truck when he was small. He felt very small right then.

He tried the hangar doors and, sure enough, they were locked tight.

The sunlight had dimmed. A clock on the wall showed the time as 5:30. His father would be closing up in a half hour, unless he'd already called home to make sure Jake had arrived safely. Maybe Mom and Dad now were driving up and down the streets, furious and scared at the same time, both yelling his name.

Fighting his fear and the urge to cry in frustration, he told himself to settle down and think. If this was a video game, how would his Space Marine escape? Look around—any doors?

He wandered the interior, trying not to get distracted by the planes and all of the cool World War II stuff the guys had stashed there: an antique bike, a parachute, heavy green fuel barrels. A banner along one wall traced the history of these planes, which were called Aircoupes. In the back of the hangar stood a two-story wooden tower painted a military-like olive drab, like a fort for GI Joe, and labeled "Tiger Flight Operations." Unfortunately, the doors downstairs and upstairs were locked.

From the second-floor landing, though, Jake could see across the hangar to the side with the high-up windows, through which he saw the road that would lead him home. Along the wall below the windows sat stacks and stacks of cylinders the size of tall paint cans, also colored olive drab. It looked like the only way out would be through the glass.

Jake scrambled down the stairs and glanced once more at the clock on the wall. 5:41. Yikes! He dashed over to the windows to give them a closer look. The center portion of each one appeared to have a lever, with a hinge set in the frame. Okay, finally he was getting a break. Too bad the bottom edge of each panel was six feet off the ground. Even if he could jump and hang on to the ledge, he wouldn't have a free hand to open the glass.

Time to build some steps. The cans might do the trick. The Tiger Flight guys would realize someone had gotten into, and broke out of, their hangar, but they wouldn't know it was him. Fearing that the big man with the mustache would return any second, he got busy.

Yellow stenciling labeled each can as "LUBRICATING OIL AIRCRAFT PISTON ENGINE." A handle on the top of each one enabled him to heave it into place as he created a staircase leading up to the window. With the last one set on top, Jake stood on his makeshift steps, grimy from the oil residue and dust, and tried the window lever.

He couldn't budge it.

Either the lever was stuck or somehow locked in place. Jake peered hard at the mechanism, his eyesight now well adjusted to the dimming light, and saw the flip-lock. He pushed it with his thumb but it didn't move. Shoot!

From his vantage point, he could see the road that would lead him back to the highway and to home. But here he was, stuck on a stack of lubricating oil cans. Wait…"lubricating"? That's what he and Dad once did with his bike chain so it would glide smoothly around the sprockets.

He gritted his teeth and, with a grunt, managed to unscrew the tight cap from the can beneath his feet. Dipping in his longest two fingers, he felt cool, slick liquid cover them. He slathered the brown oil over the locking mechanism and, with his dry hand, worked the lever back and forth. Hopefully the oil would slip in and do its job.

Jake tried again. It creaked and gave a little. He slammed it with the heel of his hand and the lock clicked open. Yes!

When he turned the handle, the glass panel swung outward on creaking hinges and he nearly tumbled out. He looked down at the long, long drop to the concrete. Far below, his bike still leaned against the wall. Too bad this wasn't a cowboy movie; his bike would be a horse he could whistle for, and then he'd leap down onto it and ride into the sunset.

He had a bad feeling that a jump this far might break his legs or at least sprain an ankle. Then he couldn't cycle home. He needed a rope.

His thoughts drifted back to the parachute hanging on the outside of the Tiger Flight Operations building. Leaving the window open, he scampered down the step-like cans and sprinted across the hangar. The clock showed the time as 5:59. When he got home he was done for, but first he had to escape this trap. Then his folks could punish him. So that's what "out of the frying pan, into the fire" meant.

Grabbing fistfuls of the parachute cord, he gave a yank and heard the ripping of silk as the top of the chute tore away from a pair of hooks. He was through with being stealthy—the only thing that mattered was to get out.

He bundled the smooth, musty fabric in his arms and ran behind the tiger-striped planes, back to his staircase. Even in passing, the Aircoupes looked magical. The daydreamer in him wanted to stay and climb back inside the cockpit. The realist told the daydreamer, "You're nuts." Still, Jake hoped he could see the planes again one day. Out in the open.

Crouching near the base of the aluminum wall, he tied one end of the chute to a rusty bolt that emerged from the metal. Jake mounted his makeshift steps, letting the fabric and cords trail away as he climbed. He tossed the remaining length of worn, yellowed silk through the open window, and tried not to think about the awful things that would happen to him if the parachute shredded like cobwebs when he put his weight on it.

Jake paused to take a last look at the planes. He hated to say goodbye.

He gripped the ancient, frayed lifeline and swung his legs through the open window. The oil staining his hand probably would leave fingerprints. Could they somehow lead the police to him? So much to worry about.

Backing out, he banged his head on the top of the window frame. To his surprise, he really did see stars. Woozy now as well as panicked and exhausted, he put his weight on the chute and started his descent. From inside, a slow ripping sound filled him with dread. He climbed down faster than he'd ever done anything in his life. All at once, the silk tore free from the bolt.

Jake dropped only a short distance, but the sudden freefall scared him as he tumbled backward onto the asphalt. The parachute settled over his head and body. For an instant he felt like a commando who had just dropped behind enemy lines.

Snapping out of his fantasy, he balled up the fabric, wrapped the cord around it, and pitched the bulky wad through the open window high over his head. Two points!

Then he remembered the fingerprints. Too late now.

He raced to his bike. With a deep breath, he spun it around and pumped hard, standing on the pedals as he shot down the road toward the highway.

Instead of congratulating himself on his escape, he imagined the lectures and punishments that awaited him. Grounded for life, no TV, only veggies and water from now on. Each new penalty made him pedal faster. Still, the suffering would be worth it—those planes, oh man, those planes were really amazing.

To save time, he created shortcuts as he went, cutting diagonally across corner lots, looking ahead to pick the yards without fences he could zip through, ripping down streets he barely recognized. It almost felt like flying.

Sweat flew from Jake's face and rapid heartbeats pounded a drum solo in his ears as he roared into the back of his neighborhood and approached his house at top speed. Ahead, a familiar truck turned the corner toward him. It was Dad's.

Ducking his head, Jake swung into a cul-de-sac, the rear of which butted up against the side of his family's property. Mercifully, the only fence this neighbor had was an electronic one for their German Shepherd, Rolf. Jake thundered up their driveway and tore through the backyard. From nowhere came a vicious snap of canine teeth. They barely missed Jake's foot. He swerved and used the last of his strength to pedal even faster. Rolf gave chase, barking and lunging at his rear tire.

Jake slalomed between the trees that screened his house. With a yelp, the guard dog stopped and retreated. The underground fence had worked, giving Rolf a shock.

Dad pulled in at the front of the house. The garage door hummed and clanked upward. Jake almost sailed into the backyard, but there sat Mom at the patio table, reading a book.

He skidded to the side of their home, out of sight. Beside the low hedge, he tumbled off the bike. Then he lay down on the grass and stared at the darkening sky, gulping air.

Around back, the sliding-glass door opened and Dad said, "Susan, have you seen Jake?"

Mom replied, "No. Wasn't he with you?"

"He was acting grumpy so I sent him home," Dad said, his voice rising in alarm. "He left the store at 4:00."

"Oh, God." Mom sounded frightened.

Before things got out of hand, Jake called out with as much whiny exasperation as he could muster, "I'm over here." He wiped the sweat from his forehead, strolled around the corner of the house, and waved his handheld as if they'd once again interrupted his battle against the Perinoxians. Trying to take slow, deep, normal breaths, he asked, "When's dinner?"

CHAPTER FIVE

Every Saturday night Jake and his folks picked a DVD to watch. The discussion at dinner played out the way it always did: action movies versus comedies versus "something serious for a change." As usual, Mom voted for a sad or romantic movie—for some reason, she liked to cry—but Jake and his dad had long ago formed a voting block that always vetoed her. Having experienced enough action for one day, Jake wanted a comedy and Dad agreed as long as he could pick it.

That meant Dad would choose one of his favorites, press Mute on the remote control at random times, and recite the dialog perfectly in the same voices as the actors. It was freaky, but Jake and his mom always laughed.

In the family room, Dad prepared to put *Young Frankenstein* in the video player but then stopped and turned to Jake, who was sitting next to his mom on the couch, already crunching his way through his first bowl of popcorn. Dad said, "We got off to a rough start today at the store. You said you'd come in tomorrow and help out again—I've changed my mind and decided to take you up on that."

Jake coughed, shooting half-chewed pieces of popcorn across the coffee table.

"Oh, gross!" Mom said. She ripped a sheet off the roll of paper towels that she kept at her side on movie night because someone always spilled something. Dropping the sheet in Jake's lap, she ordered in her ruler-of-ten-galaxies voice, "Clean that up, space cadet."

As he collected the gummy flecks, Jake said, "But, Dad, on Sundays all the guys come over for Bella Roma's pizza and video games."

His father replied, "So you weren't serious when you offered to help me?" He made it sound like an innocent question, but Jake knew it was a trap.

"Uh, sure, I was serious," Jake said, stalling. "Just let me throw this away." Taking his time to dispose of the paper towel in the kitchen, at the other end of the house, he considered his options and realized that he'd set himself up. If he'd kept his mouth shut, they'd already be watching the movie and his Sunday would go as usual: Mom ordering some pizzas from Eddie at Bella Roma around noon, and soon the cars would start dropping off his best buddy Adam and his other friends for the afternoon. It was a sweet deal, but he'd blown it.

He returned to the family room. Trying not to sound like he

was really disappointed and miserable, he said, "Yeah, sure I'll help out at the store. Don't start the movie until I send an e-mail to everybody about tomorrow." He trudged off to his bedroom like a condemned prisoner to cancel the Sunday get-together. After turning on his computer, he opened the mail program and blasted a note to the guys:

omg- dads mking me wrk in the stor 2moro!
gotta do it- wrlds gr8st son etc
c u @ skul

Dad waited for him to return to the couch before he pressed the Play button. Twenty minutes into the movie, as Dad was reciting the lines along with Dr. Frankenstein and Igor, his cell phone rang. He paused the DVD and had a halting conversation with the angry caller, Adam's father, who Adam obviously had told about Jake's e-mail—including the "making me work" part. From the way Dad kept glaring at Jake, it was clear he didn't like being blamed for ruining Adam's parents' Sunday. Apparently, they'd made anniversary plans, counting on Adam being at Jake's all afternoon.

Dad muted the phone and said to Mom, "Even though Jake will be at the store with me, can Adam come over anyway?"

"No way, no how." Mom shook her head emphatically. "This isn't a daycare center."

Dad sighed, un-muted the phone, and said, "Uh, maybe you

can still get a sitter for Adam…Sure, it'll be a one-time thing. Any other Sunday should be fine."

Jake took a keen interest in the kernels at the bottom of his popcorn bowl as Dad closed his phone with a snap like Rolf the German Shepherd's jaws. He said to Jake, "Why'd you set me up?"

"I'm sorry," Jake whined. "It's just that I didn't want the guys to blame me for ruining tomorrow."

Mom replied icily, "Are you sorry for what you did or sorry you got caught?"

"Both." The word leaped out before he had a chance to think.

Dad actually laughed a little. "Well, that was honest anyway." He switched off the TV and said, "Do you realize that we do the right thing because it's the right thing to do, not because we're afraid of getting caught doing the wrong thing?"

Jake turned over the sentence in his mind a few times and when it made sense he said, "Yes, sir."

Mom shook the paper towel roll at him. "So what's the right thing to do now?"

"Send another e-mail, I guess."

As he worked on his second message of the night—which took awhile because he was trying to be honest without admitting his lie—he heard his mom say, "I thought we were offering a safe, fun place for his friends to hang out, but people act like it's guaranteed free babysitting."

Dad said, “Well, it wasn’t my idea to start that.” Then he shouted, “Oww!”

“You’re lucky I only hit you with a roll of Bounty. I’m going to bed.” She stomped past Jake’s room and shut the master bedroom door with a thump.

The TV came on, along with the movie, but they were soon shut off again. Dad declared to himself, “Even Mel Brooks can’t make me laugh tonight.”

Everyone was angry with everyone else now, but Jake knew that mostly they were unhappy with him.

Despite everything that had gone wrong, Jake still slept soundly, lulled by exhaustion from his escape and his memories of the twin-tailed tigers flying low overhead in diamond formation, the lead pilot saluting him. The images looped over and over, and as soon as he woke up, he replayed the scene again. Really it was all he wanted to think about. He’d heard the term “obsessed” but hadn’t known what it meant until now.

Then the reality of his situation pushed aside the Tiger Flight daydreams. During their morning routines, Mom and Dad were polite to him, but also distant and cold. He knew they’d snap out of it—they always did—but the mood in the household dragged Jake down even further.

He and his dad dressed in casual clothes and headed off to the hardware store in gloomy silence. Jake carried his handheld in a front pocket just in case Dad let him take a break, but he couldn't get excited about blasting some evil squids. This realization made him even more depressed.

Shortly after they opened the store, Jake heard some men enter, heavy shoes or boots clumping on the wood floor. He resumed counting wrenches and sighing to himself.

Dad said, "Hey, guys, how are things at the airport?"

Jake's heart skipped. Was it the airport police?

"Things are weird, Nick," a man with a deep, forceful voice replied. "We had a break-in last night, but it looked more like a break-out. Whoever it was didn't take anything. Mostly he—if it was a 'he'—wanted to escape. Even tossed back the old parachute he used to climb out through a window."

Instantly, Jake's scalp prickled with sweat and his hands began to tremble. He crept along the aisles until he could spy the men through some shelves. The big, mustached man was there in his tan flight suit and black ball cap. Three men with him wore the same uniform.

Each one had a large patch on the right side of his chest that matched the Tiger Flight shield on the planes and on the banner outside the hangar. A small black rectangle over the left breast bore silver aviator wings and some writing underneath, too far away for Jake to read. Their caps had the name "TIGER FLIGHT" stitched in yellow thread.

They might not be police, but they carried themselves like

military men Jake had seen in the movies. Maybe they could arrest him anyway.

The one with the powerful voice was the tall, strong-looking man with the mustache. "There was no one in there when I shut the doors," he said, "and the security guy said he came shortly behind to lock up, so we can't figure it out."

Dad said, "At least nothing was stolen. Y'all interested in more security, maybe for the windows too? I've got a wide variety of locks over there." He pointed toward a shelf near Jake, who retreated and took up a new spying position behind a big cardboard cutout of a NASCAR driver selling paint.

Another of the pilots, a stout man with merry eyes and a wide, friendly face, said, "That's why we're here. Let's take a look at your stock." He slid on a pair of round reading glasses.

At least they hadn't gotten his fingerprints and somehow linked him to the crime. Jake wanted to relax but couldn't. He knew he should return to work and act ignorant if his father mentioned the visit. However, curiosity about the men who flew those awesome planes rooted him there, along with the unhealthy thrill of danger, like putting his hand too close to a red-hot burner.

As Dad showed them the locksets, the third pilot, who had a wiry build and dark hair curling from under his cap, said, "No, nothing was stolen, but the intruder did damage my plane. He stepped on the wing root—that's where the wing connects to the fuselage—and made a dent in it. It's a federal offense, you know, damaging an airplane."

Jake's knees began to wobble and his stomach cramped with fear. Icy sweat clawed down his sides. Could he be locked away forever? Shot by a firing squad?

The wiry pilot added, "What I can't figure out is how he didn't do more harm to that wing—a regular-sized man would've crumpled it. Either he's a small guy or it's a 'she' not a 'he.' Or maybe some kid got in there."

Brushing his mustache, the tall one said, "My money's on the midget."

The fourth pilot, who had graying hair and a rugged face that would've looked more at home under a cowboy hat instead of a ball cap, stared at the big guy like he'd beamed down from a UFO, but the cowboy remained silent.

Eyes twinkling behind his glasses, the stout man said, "I'm betting on the girl. Probably came in to find a souvenir. You know they all fall in love with us."

While the others laughed, Jake thought about running away forever. He'd never caused so much trouble in his life—and things kept getting worse and worse. Having Mrs. K send him home with a note was no big deal compared to busting up a pilot's plane and maybe going to jail. He had to decide what to do. In his mind, he heard his mom's voice: "Are you sorry for what you did or sorry you got caught?" At least he hadn't gotten caught. Yet.

The only reason he was overhearing this conversation, instead of hanging out with his friends at home, was because he'd overplayed things with Dad the day before. If only he could learn to keep his mouth shut.

He realized he kept having the same kind of problem, but not because he couldn't shut up—it was because he always made the decision to cover something up or bend the truth or flat out lie. Sometimes he even lied to himself. How could he break out of that loop and return to being the happy kid everyone liked and trusted?

As Jake went around and around with his thoughts, the tall pilot said, "The funny thing is, we've never had a problem before, in all the years we've flown with Tiger Flight."

Dad said, "Well, let's keep it from happening again. This lock here—"

"It's all my fault," Jake announced, loud and clear, while a voice in his head asked what the heck he was doing. He stepped around the paint display, once again feeling very small, as his dad and the other men turned to stare at him. His legs had turned to jelly, but he forced himself to walk up to the staring men. Ready to take his licks. To start over again. Reboot as Jake 2.0.

He took a deep, shaky breath. "I saw you fly overhead yesterday and I wanted to get another look at your planes, so when my dad let me leave early, I biked over to the airport." He inhaled again, telling himself to look at his dad and the pilots and not the wood floor. Look them in the eyes as he finally told the truth. "I opened the hangar door after you left—" he gestured to the tall man "—and then I got locked inside." He turned to the slim pilot with the dark hair. "I didn't mean to wreck your plane. I just wanted to look in the cockpit."

The man with the friendly face said, "You did a great job figuring out a way to escape, I'll give you that much. We were really impressed." His fellow pilots didn't look impressed, so he shut up.

Dad's jaws tightened as he appeared to get madder and madder. He blurted, "Besides being a flat-out stupid thing to do, don't you know how dangerous that was?"

Jake tried to guess his punishment, but each horrible fate seemed too mild as he watched his father's temper continue to rise. He said, "Sorry, Dad."

"'Sorry' isn't going to cut it," his father shot back. "Besides, you should be apologizing to these men, not to me."

Jake stood close enough now that he could read what was printed under the wings on the black aviator patch every pilot wore. In quotes was what looked like a nickname. He said to them, "I'm sorry. I really am."

Each of the men reacted differently. "Sunny," the slim, dark-haired man whose plane Jake had damaged, studied him even harder than before, as if trying to read his mind. Removing his reading glasses, "TC" gave him a noncommittal shrug. The pilot with the cowboy's face and the name of "Winder" rocked back on his heels, folded his arms, and nodded. "Fury" merely twitched his mustache. No one said, "Forget about it" or "Apology accepted," or did anything else to make Jake feel like he hadn't just made the biggest mistake of his life.

Dad spread his hands and said to the pilots, "Jake did an awful thing and I assure you he'll be punished like never before. How much is it to repair—"

Sunny held up his hand to stop Dad and said, "You know, Nick, I have to say that it takes a lot of guts to do what he just did. 'Jake,' is it?"

Jake nodded. He realized that Sunny was the lead pilot when the formation flew overhead and started this whole mess. Sunny was the one who had saluted him.

The pilot leaned down to Jake's level and talked only to him. "I'm Sunny." He pointed to his aviator patch. "It's my call sign, what everyone calls me when I'm with the Tiger Flight." He gave Jake a firm handshake. "On the one hand, I'm angry with you for damaging my plane. But, on the other hand," he added quickly, "I have to congratulate you for stepping up. You just behaved like a Pilot in Command. You took responsibility for your actions and for how they affected others." He straightened and asked the other pilots, "Don't you think so?"

Fury said to Jake, “Yeah, chief, I guess it was pretty brave, ’fessing up that way.” He put his massive fists on his hips. “I bet we looked mighty scary to you.”

“You still do,” Jake said and immediately wanted to kick himself, but the others smiled. Everyone but Dad.

TC gave Jake a thumbs up, saying, “You might be a troublemaker, but you’re also a stand-up guy.”

Winder kept his arms folded, but tilted his head to one side as if considering this statement and then nodded again, still the silent cowboy.

Sunny said, “It would’ve been a lot easier to stay hidden over there and not say a word. There’s no way anyone would’ve ever accused you, so why did you speak up?”

Jake glanced at his father and said, “My dad told me that ‘we do the right thing because it’s the right thing to do.’” This had been the notion he’d kept returning to while quaking behind the paint display. He hoped the reason he’d stepped out and “stepped up” was good enough.

“That’s mighty right,” TC said. He clapped Dad on the shoulder. “You’re doing a good job with him, Nick.”

Dad’s expression softened and he actually blushed as he murmured thanks. Speaking up, he said, “There’s still the matter of paying for the repairs to Sunny’s plane.”

For the first time, Winder spoke. “We don’t want your money,” he said and pointed at Jake. “We want him.”

Fury said, “We do?” which made TC laugh.

Winder kept his Western eyes on Jake. He asked, “Why did you get into all this trouble?”

Jake was relieved by such an easy question. “I wanted to see your really cool planes.”

Winder nodded. “Think we can trust you not to mess with them anymore?” he asked.

“I won’t get near them ever again. Promise.”

The cowboy glanced at Sunny, who said, “If it’s okay with you, Nick, Jake can work off his debt on weekends, starting next Saturday. He’ll stack cans of lubricating oil, which he’s already shown a talent for, push a broom, fetch us coffee, or whatever chore that needs doing.”

Jake’s head reeled from the turn in his luck. Saturdays at the Tiger Flight hangar? Sweet! Who knew that telling the truth—confessing—could’ve worked out so well? He couldn’t help but smile wide.

Fury said, “You’re missing the point, chief.” He loomed over Jake. “This is punishment. You’re not a volunteer hangar kid who sweeps the floor in return for getting to fly with us once in awhile. You’re grounded—in the original sense of the word—and you have a debt to work off.”

The other pilots nodded their agreement; even TC put a stern look on his face. But they were the ones who missed the point, Jake thought. Even doing the worst kind of chores all day around the hangar meant he could be near those magical planes and watch the pilots in action. He looked at his dad and mouthed, "Please, please, please?"

Dad adopted Winder's pose, weight back, arms crossed. He asked the men, "For how long? A couple of months?"

TC replied, "Three months at least." He stared down at Jake and added, "Maybe six."

Dad considered for another long moment. Finally, he said, "Well, it beats paying for a new airplane wing. Plus, maybe Jake will learn the meaning of responsibility, working for you guys on Saturdays and Sundays."

Jake swallowed hard. He hadn't realized when Sunny said "weekends" that he meant Sundays too. The guys from school would give him a terrible time. And Dad's cell phone would never stop ringing with angry calls from Adam's parents and the others who lost their "guaranteed free daycare." Everyone would be unhappy with him forever.

Before he could protest, his father said, "You're getting off easy, pal. These guys could call the police—heck, they could call the FBI—and you'd have to go to juvenile court, and maybe even jail." Dad still looked really ticked off at him. "Instead, you'll work in an interesting place and learn new things. That's a much better deal than you'll get from me," he said. "I'll have you dusting every shelf in here and polishing each nail and screw as punishment."

Jake decided that his friends would have to get over it and

find something else to do with their Sundays. Besides, how could they fault him for being a stand-up guy, a Pilot in Command?

He liked the sound of that: Jake Skyler, Pilot in Command.

Standing tall, shoulders back, he said, “I’ll do it.” Like he had a choice.

CHAPTER SIX

When Jake and his parents sat down to eat that night, Dad said, "Susan, Jake has something he wants to tell you."

Yeah, right.

In reality, Jake wanted to put his mistakes behind him and get on with being Jake 2.0, but instead he had to go through the whole thing again with Mom while their spaghetti dinner got cold on the plates in front of them.

As he reluctantly told his story, she showed the same series of emotions as his father had earlier. Shock. Anger. Disappointment. But there was something more: horror, as if her worst nightmare had come to life. Jake could see he was breaking her heart.

Surprisingly, Dad ended up playing the pilots' role, coming to his defense. Dad even used their words: "stepped up" and "stand-up guy." Not "Pilot in Command," but after all, his dad didn't talk like a pilot. Jake expected to sound just like Sunny and the others in a few weeks. First though, he had to survive his mother.

"Jake's going to get hurt at the airport," she fretted to Dad.

"He'll pick up bad habits. He'll grow up too fast." On and on she went, worrying about what Jake thought of as "mom" stuff. She talked like he wasn't sitting there.

Finally, his father pointed out, "Jake has to pay his debt. He'll definitely learn some responsibility this way."

That silenced her for a moment. Good ol' Dad.

Mom said, "Okay, you win. But I'm going with him next Saturday and check out these pilots, the hangar, the whole situation." She swiveled around to Jake and pointed her fork at him. "If I don't like what I see, we'll figure out another way for you to pay what you owe."

To Jake, this would be like his mother joining a sleepover with his coolest friends, but her crashing his party was only one of the punishments she and Dad agreed to. For his lying and all the stuff he did at the Tiger Flight hangar, they outlawed the computer, his video games, the phone, and TV for a month. An entire month—like forever! Even worse, Mom said, "Don't worry. I'll check your e-mails and tell you if someone sent anything that's important."

The thought of his mom reading messages he and his friends had sent gave Jake another round of sweating and shaking. So, the first thing he said on Monday morning before first period math class started was, "Hey, guys, don't send me any messages. I'm banned from the computer. And from TV and everything else but breathing for a whole month."

Adam had just dropped into his seat next to Jake, having

spent too much time at his locker as usual. He scratched his curly black hair and said, “A month? That’s, like, forever.”

“I know!” Jake moaned, and then lowered his voice when Mrs. Kirby shot him a look from across the room. She still held the letter his parents had signed. Mrs. K had a kind face but her glare could cut like a laser beam.

Adam, who was Jake’s best friend and constant e-mail buddy, asked, “Is your mother checking your messages?” When Jake nodded glumly, Adam said, “Uh oh. I hope she likes the Yo Mama jokes I sent you.”

“They banned you from everything?” Peter, a husky kid who was always getting too fat for his new clothes, looked concerned. He asked, “Can you eat at least?” Maybe he was thinking about life without French fries. They sat at their usual desks in the back of the room, and Jake could see a bag of chocolate candy peeking from the backpack under Peter’s chair. Not the snack size, but the bag folks buy to fill up a party bowl.

“Sure I can eat,” Jake snapped. “I can drink too.” Peter was a good guy—always the one who challenged him for the top spot at any video game—but he could be so dense sometimes. “They’ll even let me sleep, but that’s about all.”

The third member of Jake’s inner circle was Vic. Vic used terms like “inner circle” all the time, passing along his dad’s business lingo, and had started his own investment club. Jake liked him because Vic had invested Jake’s allowance money and already returned a profit of $20. Unnaturally tall and skinny, Vic loomed over the rest of them even when sitting. His voice was deep, as if it came up from his shoes. He said, "What did you do? Microwave another egg?"

Jake rolled his eyes. Adam had told Jake in second grade that microwaving an egg for a long time at low power was "like an incubator in fast-forward" and would cause a chick to hatch from the shell in minutes. Instead, it had been like a time bomb. Mom still described the incident as "the day Jake blew up the kitchen."

He said, "You guys gotta promise not to tell anyone."

"Hold on," Vic said, opening his laptop. Jake always thought that was a little weird, bringing his own laptop to sixth grade. Vic swirled his finger on the touch pad. "I think my dad gave me a nondisclosure agreement we can all sign."

"A what?" Adam raised his fist to Vic. "I'm gonna give your computer a five-fingered reboot if you don't quit it." The jock of the bunch, Adam could probably bust a hole through the screen.

"Adam," Mrs. K called out, "are you threatening Victor?"

"No, ma'am. We were, uh, just playing rock, paper, scissors." He showed her his fist. "I'm the rock."

"Rocks in the head," Peter whispered.

Mrs. K waved Jake's letter at Adam. "Paper smothers rock. Make sure you don't go home with one of these too."

"Yes, ma'am." Adam slammed the laptop screen down, almost catching Vic's long fingers. "Enough screwing around. Jake, what did you do?"

A girl's voice said, "He stepped on an airplane wing and dented it."

They all turned to where Debra sat in the far corner. Jake had always figured her for a front-row brainiac, since she got good grades and every teacher loved her, but for some reason she liked to hang out in the back where the slackers, goofballs, and class clowns slouched.

Jake said, "What are you, psychic? How do you know?"

"My uncle Max is the Tiger Flight mechanic. He was having dinner with me and my folks when he got a call from Sunny about the wing."

Peter asked, "Who's Sunny?" as Adam and Vic both said, "Airplane wing?"

Jake decided he hated Debra. Obviously she'd known about the Tiger Flight long before him. She had probably even flown in their planes after Uncle Max repaired them. He thought the Tiger Flight was his secret and it turned out to be hers. There she sat, pretending to be innocent but having all the answers before the questions were even asked. She was so irritating.

Vic said, "Did the pilots have insurance? Are they going to sue you?" He opened his laptop again, murmuring, "Indemnification...."

Adam slammed it shut once more. "Jake—tell us what happened." He ignored Debra, as always. Everything she said or did got under his skin. Now Jake could understand why.

The warning bell rang, so they only had a few minutes before class would start. He took a breath and told the story.

At the end, Adam whined, "So we can't come over anymore on Sundays?" His fists clenched. He looked furious enough to rip a book—or Jake—in half.

Jake said, "That's all you care about? My whole life has changed and you can only think of where you're gonna play video games on Sundays?"

"And eat pizza," Peter added. If anything, he looked more upset than Adam, but sad, not angry. And a little hungry.

Vic moved his laptop out of Adam's reach and began clicking open files. "You might need a good lawyer."

Jake grumbled, "What I need is another bunch of friends. Guys who'll stick with me."

Debra said, "I think you did a really courageous thing, speaking up because it was the right thing to do."

Vic countered, "It would've been smarter to obey his dad and go straight home."

"Enough," Adam snarled. "The point you're missing is that Jake screwed up Sundays for everyone because he blabbed to his dad and those pilots. Why can't you learn to just shut up?"

Somehow Adam's comments stung more than all of the

other abuse heaped on him in the past few days. His best friend had turned against him, and the only one who'd stick up for him was a girl.

"I'll be your friend." The wormy voice came from two rows up. Matt the Armpit was beaming at Jake. The kid didn't wear mere glasses—those things on his face were goggles. He could probably attach windshield wipers to them. His nose was always running, and his hair looked like he combed it with a tree branch. And he never took a bath. The kids all said Matt was "backwards," because his nose ran and his feet smelled instead of the other way around. The worst thing, though, was that sniveling, needy, creepy-crawly voice.

Friends with Matt. Great.

"I'll be your friend too." From near the front of the class came a dead-on impression of Matt, so perfect it sounded like an echo. Of course. Billy Grant did everything perfectly. He'd never gotten a wrong answer in the six years Jake had known him. Blond and blue-eyed, a kid so good-looking that girls in eighth grade stared at him. His rich parents dressed him in the hippest clothes; whatever Billy wore, everyone wanted to wear the same. As soon as they did, he switched styles and watched everybody struggle to catch up. He always had the latest movies, the best game console, the tiniest cell phone. Billy had a wireless earpiece when most people thought Bluetooth was a dental disease. Friends with Billy Grant—now that was more like it.

Jake said, "Really?"

Billy sneered, showing perfect white teeth, and laughed out loud.

CHAPTER SEVEN

When Jake saw the Tiger Flight pilots on Saturday morning, he thought that even Billy Grant would've been envious of them. Those guys were so confident they didn't need to swagger; they just knew they could do whatever needed to be done.

Behind him, Mom said, "Wow," but maybe she was only responding to the four tiger-striped planes they'd rolled from the hangar into the warm morning sunlight.

Sunny waved to Jake and his mom and marched over, dressed in his tan flight suit, black Tiger Flight cap, and black lace-up boots. "Mrs. Skyler," he said, shaking her hand.

"Uh, call me Susan. Please." She sounded edgy, like she was ready to bolt for the car.

"I'm Sunny."

"Like 'bright and sunny'?" she asked. When he nodded and pointed to his aviator patch, she said, "Does everyone here go by a nickname?"

Jake said, "They're not nicknames, Mom. They're call

signs. Everybody knows that."

Sunny explained, "It's an aviator tradition—sometimes even the ground crew gets them."

Mom patted Jake's back, which embarrassed him so much he thought he'd shrivel up and die. His mother had been patting him all morning, like he was going away and she'd never see him again. She said, "Will you pick out a call sign for Jake?"

"They sort of pick themselves out, you can't force it. Sooner or later Jake will do or say something, or he'll act a certain way, and—bingo—we'll know what his call sign should be." He looked at Jake, sizing him up again as he'd done in the hardware store. "The guys have tossed around a couple of ideas but nothing's stuck yet."

Mom looked past him at the other pilots, who were busy inspecting their planes. They moved with brisk steps, all business. She said, "Your group—"

"Flight, Mom. It's the Tiger *Flight*," Jake said. He was increasingly afraid she'd insult Sunny and blow the whole deal.

"Your *flight*," she emphasized, "seems to be in a hurry."

Sunny said, "We use the first flight of the day to make sure all systems are go. Then, it's the kids' turn."

"Oh?" Mom's fingernails dug into Jake's shoulder.

Sunny said, "We're initiating a Young Eagles program, starting today. Parents can sign a consent form and we'll fly their kids for free."

"Free airplane rides?" Jake shouted. "Cool."

"We're all members of this group called EAA, which created the program. You know Harrison Ford? He's the Chairman of the EAA Young Eagles Program—even he flies kids around."

Before Jake could get excited about the idea of flying with Indiana Jones, Mom said, "But Jake isn't going to go up, right?"

"That's right. He's here to pay off a debt, not to have fun. When he's done that, then we'll see."

"We'll see, but I don't think so," Mom stated in a flat voice. Then, as if afraid she'd been rude, she added, "Sorry, I've always been a little concerned about flying."

Sunny shrugged. "If and when he does go up, you have nothing to worry about. Tiger Flight pilots have a combined 70,000 hours in the air."

"It's not you," she reassured him. "It's me. A mother always worries. That's my call sign: Worrywart." She chuckled nervously. Jake stared up at her. Someone had swapped his imperial queen, ruler of ten galaxies, with a Nervous Nellie.

She stroked his neck, further humiliating him. "I'm glad Jake's working for you now instead of sneaking around here. At least he won't have to break out of your building anymore."

"Mom," Jake grumbled, "it's called a hangar."

He rolled his eyes to show Sunny how mortified he was at her odd behavior and lack of the most basic aviator vocabulary.

The pilot pointed at him and said, "Hey, show some respect."

Jake stammered through an apology, staring at his shoes, suddenly worried *he* was going to blow the whole deal.

Sunny addressed Mom again, saying, "If we lock him in the hangar again, Susan, it'll be because you told us to."

Mom smiled, actually relaxing a little, and the mood lightened. Sunny led them over to TC, Winder, and Fury and introduced her. All of the pilots acted as polite and respectful as King Arthur's knights. The word "chivalrous," which Jake remembered from his book on Camelot, fit them nicely.

They returned to inspecting their planes, and Sunny took Jake and his mom on a tour of the hangar, including Jake's staircase of oilcans and the two-story Tiger Flight Operations tower, which was now unlocked.

The first floor, called the Ready Room, contained a whiteboard, like at school, along with aluminum chairs that had each pilot's call sign on the back—including one for some pilot named "Bones." In the Ready Room, the pilots conducted their briefings to decide on the flight plan for the day, agree on the radio frequencies they'd use for communications, and remind each other of the formations and maneuvers they wanted to practice. As Sunny explained all of this, Jake inspected the dozens of model planes hanging from the ceiling, the World War II bunk beds along one wall, and other WWII gear and posters. He drifted into a daydream of the model planes coming to life and battling each other overhead with machine guns and bombs. Mom had to call his name to get his attention and tell him they were going upstairs.

The second level housed the Pilots Lounge, with tables and chairs and a mini-fridge from which Sunny poured each of them a soda. Outside, the engines started with throaty rumbles, and TC, Fury, and Winder taxied toward the runway. The growl of their planes grew ever fainter until they faded completely. Jake imagined himself relaxing at one of the tables later, leaning his chair on its back legs, head propped against the wall, as he listened to the pilots tell awesome stories about their flying adventures.

Back in the warm sunshine, Mom took forever to look over Sunny's plane, asking a bazillion questions. Adding to Jake's embarrassment, she studied the spot on the wing root where Jake had stepped, which Debra's uncle Max had made like new. And then Mom had to make sure—yet again—that Jake was grounded and wouldn't be flying. What was up with her?

She told Jake she would pick him up at 4:30, and she drove off at last. As soon as her car turned away from them in the parking lot, Jake stopped waving and said to Sunny, "Sorry about my mom. She can be such a *mom*, you know?"

"She's got a tough job," Sunny replied. "All you have to do is look after yourself, but parents have to make sure they stay safe *and* keep their kids out of trouble too. And that's impossible because your parents can't be around you all the time." He sounded stern, in full Lecture Mode. "Which is why you're here in the first place."

As Mom's car traveled down the road leading back to the highway, Sunny's tone became even more serious. "What I told you about being a Pilot in Command, responsible for yourself and others? That's your mom and dad: Pilots in Command of their lives. Good thing for you to remember, Jake."

CHAPTER EIGHT

Still standing in the airport parking lot, Sunny detailed Jake's first duties: sweep out the hangar and restack the oilcans the way they were before he turned them into a staircase. Jake had a feeling he was going to have to deal with the cans again. He asked, "Will I have to clean and fix the parachute I tore?"

"No, we re-hung it so the grease and rips don't show." He led Jake back toward the hangar. "In the afternoon, when we're finished flying the Young Eagles, you'll wash and wax a couple of the planes and do the others on Sunday." With a humorless chuckle, he added, "We'll show you where to step."

Jake's heart leaped. He'd expected the pilots to bar him from coming anywhere near the planes. Unable to contain his enthusiasm, he said, "That sounds great."

"Maybe with the first one or two," Sunny said, "but wait until you're wet and tired and there's still Tiger 4 to do. Remember, kid, this is payback time and we intend to work you hard."

When they returned to the Tiger Flight hangar, TC, Fury,

and Winder were still airborne. Sunny's plane waited in the sun, a crouching tiger poised to roar and take off. The knowledge that Jake had damaged such a beautiful thing was still a fresh scar—he didn't know if it would ever heal. Silently, he promised the plane that he would baby it from now on.

Beside one of the massive hangar doors stood a pair of clean-cut teenagers—one black and one white—talking in low tones. The white guy, who was about sixteen, stood very tall and looked as strong as a college football player. He leaned down to talk to his friend, who was maybe fifteen. They both wore black tee shirts with their name on the left side and a Tiger Flight patch on the right, olive drab pants, and black boots. On their heads were black baseball caps with yellow stitching that read "TIGER FLIGHT CREW."

As soon as the teens saw Sunny, they drew themselves up straight, like soldiers coming to attention. The new posture pulled their shirts tight against their brawny chest and arms—these boys worked out. A lot. At first Jake thought the gleam in their eyes came from a shared joke. Maybe a smile they were holding back. As he studied their identical expressions though, he decided it was a look of pride. They knew they were doing something way cool and they loved it. Jake envied them even more than he coveted Billy Grant's style, smarts, and good looks.

Sunny said, "Jake, I want to introduce you to our crewmembers. These guys are our safety officers; they keep the planes, and the people around them, safe. This is Gabriel," he said, and the black teen stepped forward and shook Jake's hand with a strong grip. "And this is Drew." The other crewmember gave Jake an equally confident handshake and stepped back with military crispness.

Sunny continued, "You'll sometimes hear the pilots refer to Gabriel by his call sign: 'Angel.' Drew keeps outgrowing his call signs. How big are you now, Drew?"

"Six-foot-three, two hundred and fifteen pounds. I just moved up to size thirteen shoes."

Sunny whistled. He told Jake, "He's outgrown the planes too—he's too tall, even with the seat pushed all the way back. But he keeps showing up here and doing his job, even if he can't fit in the cockpit anymore."

There it was again, Jake thought. Finish what you start; follow through.

Sunny announced to the crew, "Jake here is working for Tiger Flight for a while."

Gabriel nodded and smiled. "That's cool. You got a new hangar kid."

"No," Sunny said. "He damaged my plane—by accident, fooling around on it—and we thought the best way to pay us back was for him to work around us, and you guys too. You know, learn respect for the aircraft, responsibility, and a few other things."

Drew pulled the brim of his cap lower over his eyes and stared down, down, down at Jake. He said, "That's a federal crime, busting up a plane." Obviously the teen took this news personally, as if Jake had broken something of his. *Taking ownership*, Dad once had called it.

Sunny said, "Yeah, we've been over that. He's sorry, so we're giving him a chance to make amends." He checked his watch. "The first of the Young Eagles will be here in an hour, so I gotta do my preflight and get in the air. Give him the safety lecture and make sure he repeats everything twice."

The pilot hustled over to his plane, out of sight of Jake, who wanted to watch the preflight. Instead, he faced two muscular guys—one of them a giant—giving him the evil eye. He needed to show them that he cared about the planes as much as they did. They looked at him like he was Matt the Armpit; he wanted to prove that he could be another Billy Grant. Just being Jake Skyler wouldn't cut it with this crowd.

Gabriel said out of the corner of his mouth, "Does he talk?"

Drew replied, "Not a word. Maybe this is Winder's nephew or something."

"No," Gabriel huffed. "Anybody related to Winder would know how to take care of a plane from birth. It'd be in his genes."

Jake tried to mimic their military stance. He took a breath and said, "I'm really sorry I dented Sunny's wing."

Gabriel said, "He talks."

Drew responded, "Mm-hm," and still looked angry.

"He's really sorry," Gabriel added.

"Sure," Drew said, and Jake realized they were trying to scare him. It was working, a little. Drew asked, "So, can we order him around, like, forever?"

"At least until he works off his debt."

Drew grunted. Then, in a voice loud enough for Sunny and probably all of Rome to hear, he said, "Okay, Jake, here are the rules. Like Sunny said, repeat them twice so we'll know you heard them. Rule number one: no running."

"No running."

Gabriel took on Drew's drill-sergeant voice: "Louder."

"No running!"

"No horseplay, " Gabriel said.

When Jake repeated it twice, Drew commanded, "Stay away from the propellers even when they're not spinning."

It was harder to repeat a long sentence, but Jake managed to get it right.

As if to give him a small break, Gabriel pointed at Sunny's plane. "Yo, Jake. See how we keep the propeller straight up and down? That's so no one bangs into the blades by accident."

Jake turned to glance at the prop and to watch Sunny, who was checking the back portion of the wings to make sure they moved easily. Sunlight burnished the deep orange paint and made the black stripes move again—the tiger was waking and stretching. The underside glowed with the color of milk. And the two tails made the aircraft look as unique as an alien spaceship.

Drew snapped his fingers as loud as a cap pistol. "The lecture's not over, Jake."

Feeling more and more like a recruit being tested in one of those army movies, Jake recited the other safety rules twice: Listen carefully for the pilot's instructions when anywhere near a plane. Don't touch any part of the plane without the pilot's permission. Pay attention to the ground crewmembers too—they're there to keep everyone safe.

He had a feeling that they'd saved that one for last because they made him say it especially loud.

Gabriel looked past Jake and said, "Okay, worker bee, it's show time. Move off to the side and we'll show you how we get things done." He squared his shoulders even more and marched to the plane, where Sunny now sat in the cockpit.

Sunshine glinted on the clear canopy, and Jake again gazed at the beautiful tiger-striped paint. The feeling he'd had when he snuck into the hangar—the excitement of being near the plane—had grown even stronger. It was like falling under a spell.

Gabriel ducked around the propeller, yanked the orange wedge from in front of and behind the nose wheel, stepped back twenty feet, and dropped the rope-linked wooden chocks behind him. He stood at attention beside Drew, both models of proud flight crewmembers.

Sunny shouted, "Clear."

Gabriel gave the thumbs up, his arm ramrod straight in front of him. Sunny started the engine. The motor roared to life, and carbon blew out from twin pipes under the engine compartment. In an instant, the propeller became a blur and actually appeared to turn in the opposite direction for a second. The yellow spiral on the nose cone spun hypnotically.

Sunny put on his headset, pulled the microphone close to his mouth, and closed the canopy over his head. The twin-tailed tiger slid past, and Gabriel gave him a sharp salute followed by another thumbs up. Sunny responded in kind and then headed toward the taxiway, picking up speed. It took all Jake's willpower not to run after the aircraft, to try to keep pace until it took off.

When the noise faded, Drew said, "Looks like our worker has got the flying bug."

Gabriel didn't take his gaze off the receding aircraft. "I'm liking him better already."

Jake shaded his eyes with both hands as he watched Sunny's plane zoom along the sun-drenched concrete. Even far away the engine sounded powerful. Faster and faster the aircraft sped, and then—magic. When it seemed like the plane would just keep rocketing across the ground like a sports car, its nose suddenly lifted and the wheels spun without anything under them, and Jake rose on his tiptoes. Sunny was flying.

Briefly, Jake felt himself take off too.

The plane gained altitude quickly, banked far overhead, and flew directly above the Tiger Flight hangar. Sunny waggled his wings. Jake waved as the plane rose higher and headed into the sunshine.

Beside him, Drew picked up on his feeling of disappointment. The big guy said, "It's sort of sad, realizing you're not up there with him. Nothing worse than being earthbound when all you want to do is fly."

CHAPTER NINE

Jake pushed the red-bristled broom across the hangar floor, glancing up every few seconds to read the World War II posters and other memorabilia on the interior walls. A plane occasionally roared overhead. The echoing sound added to the fantasy that he worked on an airbase where brave souls took to the skies to battle evil and return as heroes.

Gabriel and Drew stood in the shade near the hangar opening. Without the planes for them to guide, they fell into the habits of regular teenagers, bantering and teasing each other. Snatches of their conversation drifted back to Jake as he guided the push broom.

Drew said to Gabriel, "Man, it sounds like you got yourself a girlfriend."

"Shoot." Gabriel shoved playfully at Drew, which was like trying to move Lavender Mountain. "I got no time for that." He glanced around and met Jake's eye. "How 'bout you? You got a girlfriend?"

Jake continued to sweep so they wouldn't accuse him of slacking off. He said, "I hardly even know any girls."

Drew said, "You go to an all-boys school?"

"No, there are girls in my classes, but I don't talk to…well, there's one—"

"Aha!" Gabriel pounced, flashing his teeth. "What's her name?"

Jake said, "Debra Mackenzie, but she's not—"

"Debra Mackenzie?" Drew repeated. "Her brother's the fullback on my team—tough as nails and smart too. Isn't their uncle the Tiger Flight mechanic?"

Gabriel said, "You mean Max? Yeah, you're right. Small world." He crossed his arms and leaned against the hangar wall. "So, Jake and Debra Mackenzie…mm-mm-mm."

Jake sputtered, "She's just this girl who sits beside me in math class."

Drew barked, "Don't stop sweeping. Work off your debt, kid." He looked pleased to have caught Jake.

A bulldog of a man, only Gabriel's height but as muscular as Drew, quick-stepped into the hangar. He wore the flight suit of a Tiger Flight pilot, but Jake hadn't seen him before. His aviator patch bore the call sign "Bones." Light flashed off his sunglasses. In a gruff voice, he asked the crewmembers, "They taking up Young Eagles already?"

"No, sir," Drew said. "The kids won't get here for another thirty minutes."

Bones looked relieved. Perspiration dampened the short, dark hair on his round head. He said, "Good thing I left the hospital when I did." Noticing Jake, he said, "We got a new hangar kid?"

Gabriel answered, "He ranks below that, just a worker. You heard about Sunny's wing getting dinged up? He's the one that did it."

Jake took a step back. The broom didn't offer any protection. Bones looked like he could snap it into matchsticks.

The burly man strode up to Jake. "You're the one who got locked in here?" He glanced at the lubricating-oil cans, the makeshift staircase still leading up to the window. "We started calling that 'The Great Escape,' after the movie, you know?"

Jake had watched it once with his dad. Come to think of it, he'd felt like Steve McQueen roaring toward freedom when he made his getaway on his bike.

He began to smile, but Bones looked deadly serious. Jake took another step back, keeping the broom between them. Bones said, "Relax, kid. I'm a physician—I don't hurt people, I heal them."

"A doctor?" Jake tried to wrap his mind around it: a doctor-pilot.

Drew said proudly, "Bones is our flight surgeon. He's also an anesthesiologist at the hospital and a major in the Army."

That awed Jake even more. A doctor-pilot-soldier. It was

like three whole lives rolled into one. He hadn't realized that a single person could do so many things.

"Don't look so impressed," Bones quipped. "These guys brag on me too much. What's your name, kid?"

"Jake. Jake Skyler."

"They call me Bones, short for 'Sawbones'—old military nickname for a doctor. I wish I could get over here more often, but I'm on call at the hospital a lot and then there's the Army duty." He checked his watch. "The flight ought to be coming in soon. Let's get the radio and I'll give you the play-by-play about what they're doing."

The doctor-pilot-soldier retrieved a portable radio from the Ready Room and motioned for Jake to follow him outside. Jake gratefully left his broom behind. He tried not to look smug as he passed the teens. It was a good thing, since they followed. Soon everyone had crowded around the man.

Bones positioned Jake in front of the group. The doctor-pilot-soldier pointed over his shoulder, toward the horizon, and said, "You see them? They'll be moving from fingertip into right echelon formation."

Sure enough, the Tiger Flight was streaking across the sky in a V-like pattern. Glancing at his right hand, fingers straight out and held together, Jake could see how the fingertip formation got its name.

Then the two planes to the right of the lead aircraft moved

farther right and the wingman on the lead's left eased behind and slid in front of the other two. The four planes now formed a tight diagonal line. This transition from fingertip to right echelon happened so smoothly that Jake could hardly believe men were steering machines up there—it looked as natural and effortless as geese in flight. Giddy tingling rose in his stomach and goosebumps spread over his arms and down his back. The sight made him so excited he bounced up and down on his toes.

Bones said, "Yeah, I still get that way too. Look, even Angel's grinning like a kid on Christmas."

Jake caught Gabriel's smile before the teen put on a more serious expression. As Jake continued to watch him though, the broad grin came out of hiding again.

Bones switched on the radio and fiddled with the tuner for a moment before locking in on the correct frequency. Winder's rock-steady voice came through the speaker. "Rome area traffic, Tiger Flight, four aircraft, turning in on the 45 for left downwind, Runway One, Rome."

Jake held his breath as the planes overflew the airfield at 120 miles per hour. Only four feet separated one wingtip from the other. It happened so fast. He wanted more time to admire their control. Behind him, Drew whistled, low and sort of sad, still wishing he was up there. Jake wished that for himself. How long would it take to pay off his debt so maybe he'd get a chance?

Over the radio, Winder said, "Rome area traffic, Tiger Flight, four aircraft, initial approach, midfield break back to the downwind, Runway One, Rome."

Bones said, "The other pilots are watching Winder the whole time. He signals them and they key off what he does. You can imagine it: he's raising his right hand high inside his canopy and twirling his index finger upright like a mini tornado. Now he's held up some fingers—two, three, or four—to tell the others how many seconds to wait before each one turns after him. Then he salutes, and there he goes!"

The lead plane snapped off a tight turn to the left. Sunlight flashed across the top of Winder's plane. Wings, fuselage, and tail fins all blazed orange and black.

Bones said, "Count, Jake: one Mississippi, two Mississippi, three Mississippi—"

Tiger 2 turned to follow Winder. Jake counted again and Tiger 3 broke left after three seconds. Like clockwork, Tiger 4 followed suit. The planes banked in a graceful curve back toward the airfield.

Winder's voice again came over the radio: "Rome area traffic, Tiger Flight, four aircraft, turning base final, full stop, Runway One, Rome."

Jake asked, "Why does he keep saying 'Rome' twice?"

Bones replied, "Because pilots from other airports could be on the same frequency that we use, and they can hear our transmissions. If someone tunes in late, he'll hear the second 'Rome,' so he knows not to look for four planes landing at *his* airport."

Winder led the others down to the tarmac, landing on one side with Tiger 2 touching down three seconds later on the other side. In another three seconds, Tiger 3 put his wheels to the blacktop behind Winder in Tiger 1. Finally, Tiger 4 eased onto the runway as soft as sliding a hand over the page of a book, trailing Tiger 2.

Winder announced, "Rome area traffic, Tiger Flight, four aircraft, clear Runway One, Rome," and guided them back to the taxiway. They paused there and then rolled toward the hangar, still in straight-line formation with each plane ten feet from the one in front of it.

Bones handed the radio to Jake before following Drew and Gabriel into position in front of the hangar. The two teens and the doctor-pilot-soldier spread out in a line as if they were in formation too. When the planes turned in unison and edged toward a yellow stripe on the concrete, Bones and the ground crew held their arms up as if signaling a touchdown and then beckoned the planes closer to the line. Jake wanted to stand in front of Tiger 4 and do the same, but he knew it wasn't his place. Maybe one day, when he wasn't just a worker, but not now.

Bones and the crewmembers crossed their forearms overhead in an X, and the planes stopped in a perfect row, engines rumbling and propellers still a blur. Nothing could look as beautiful.

Gabriel and Drew and Bones now stood at parade rest, but were still attentive. Obviously the show wasn't over. The other pilots' heads turned toward Tiger 1, still watching the lead. Winder slashed his index finger across his throat. He tapped the top of his head, as if to signal "look at me," and gave an exaggerated nod. The pilots immediately shut down their engines. The noise died and the propellers slowed to a standstill.

Winder showed a thumbs up and the others responded. Jake was so caught up in the choreography that he did it too. Simultaneously, the pilots unlocked their canopies and slid them back. Like a drill team they all stood and climbed onto their wings and then down to the concrete. They marched as precisely as they flew and met in the center to shake hands. Then Winder nodded and all four pilots strode more casually over to Bones.

TC asked the doctor-pilot-soldier, "How'd we look?"

"Together and tight," came the respectful reply.

Fury pumped his fist, and TC said, "Awright!"

Winder led the pilots, including Bones, into the Ready Room. When the door closed, Jake asked Gabriel, "What happens now?"

"Debriefing after the flight." Gabriel grabbed two sets of rope-linked chocks from the concrete, Drew picked up the other two pairs, and they set about securing the nose wheel of each plane with an orange wedge in front of and behind the tire. As they worked, Gabriel added, “The lead—Winder this time—is telling each pilot what he did well and what he’s gotta improve, if anything.”

Jake looked back to the olive-drab exterior of the Ready Room, wishing he could hear through walls. In a hushed voice, he asked, “Do they fight about it?”

“Never,” Drew said, ducking behind the propeller of Tiger 4 and sliding the chocks into place. “Whatever the lead says goes. If the Pilot in Command tells you that you screwed up, then you screwed up.”

“Kinda like with my teachers,” Jake said. “Or my parents.”

Gabriel said, “You got it.”

It occurred to Jake that the reason he was even talking to the crewmembers was because he’d screwed up. That he’d just witnessed the amazing skill and discipline of the Tiger Flight in action must’ve been what his folks called a silver lining.

In this case, he thought with a smile, the lining was tiger orange.

CHAPTER TEN

Unfortunately, watching the Tiger Flight was as close as Jake got to the action. His role as worker meant that he wasn't allowed near the planes except to wash and wax them. Worse, the pilots didn't speak to him much, and when they did it was to tell him what to do next. "When you're on the job, chief," Fury explained, "you're expected to work. Pay your debt."

Neither was Jake allowed to interact with the Young Eagles or their parents—Gabriel and Drew claimed that privilege, which Jake supposed they'd earned. And when the crew wasn't helping the visitors, the pilots were giving their guests a speech on safety, the history of aviation, their twin-tailed tiger aircraft and their connection with the original Flying Tigers of World War II, as well as some of the science of flying. By the time a few weekends had passed, Jake had heard the speech often enough that he thought he could give it himself.

It had pained him to watch the Tiger Flight passengers, some as young as eight, others as old as seventeen, deplane with big smiles and bouncy steps. Each one would eventually lift their faces to the sky as if they couldn't wait to go up again. Even the too-cool-to-care teenagers were pumped.

Seeing their reactions reminded Jake of a plaque mounted in the hangar, which all the pilots had signed. The plaque quoted Leonardo da Vinci. Because Jake and his classmates had to practice memorization so much, no matter where he was he could see da Vinci's words as if he held the plaque in his hands: "For once you have tasted flight, you will forever walk the Earth with your eyes turned skyward, for there you have been and there you long to return."

The Young Eagles testified to that, every one of them.

But Jake wasn't a Young Eagle. He wasn't even a hangar kid. He had to be content with paying off his debt and watching it all from the sidelines. Even so, he still thought about flying each night before he went to sleep, and woke up with those same fantasies. He might've been barred from the skies, but no one could deny him his dreams.

When he griped about staying earthbound while everyone around him got to fly, his friends at school didn't want to hear it. They still resented having their Sundays ruined. Only Debra asked him about what he did and saw at the hangar, which aggravated Adam even more.

Jake's mom seemed happy with the way things had worked out—his complaints to her about not going up only made her smile with relief. The strange thing was, he never saw any of the Young Eagles' parents look anything but excited for their kids. He wondered if his mother had some kind of bad experience in the past.

At least she didn't go on and on about her worries anymore. Maybe that was progress.

One Saturday, a month after he'd begun his work at the hangar, he opened the car door in the airport parking lot and was surprised that Mom didn't get out too.

When he looked back inside at her, she shrugged and said, "Work hard."

"You're not gonna grill the pilots about how I'm doing?"

"No need," she said. "They keep saying that you're doing a good job. And they've assured me you won't be flying. So say hello to them for me and I'll get you at 4:30."

Although he'd hated the walk to the hangar beside his mom, now that he did it alone he sort of missed her. He liked that she cared—not that he'd admit it to anyone. No way, never ever.

He arrived in time to see Drew and Gabriel wave in the four planes and signal them to a halt. The Tiger Flight had practiced their formation flying earlier than usual. In the cockpits today were TC, Sunny, Fury, and Bones. Winder flew for a big commercial airline, so he was probably jetting three hundred passengers to the Bahamas or some other exotic place.

After the pilots double-timed it into their debriefing, Jake asked the crewmembers, "What's the rush today?"

Drew said, "Lots of Young Eagles on the way."

Gabriel added, "First, some VIPs."

"Very important people?" Jake asked.

"Very influential politicians." Gabriel took two sets of orange chocks and followed Drew, who secured the front wheels of Tiger 1 and Tiger 2. They turned the propellers straight up and down and inspected the cockpits to make sure everything was clean and ready for the Tiger Flight passengers.

Jake busied himself in the hangar. His job that morning was to do touch-up painting on the interior where oil cans and other items had marked the walls. He knew he'd contributed to those scars during what Bones had called The Great Escape, so he couldn't complain.

In no time, pale yellow smears tattooed his arms, face, and the raggedy shirt and jeans his mother suggested that he wear. Somehow she knew he'd make a mess.

The pilots were refueling their planes in the mid-morning sun when Gabriel called to them, "Some fancy cars are pulling into the lot."

TC, Fury, and the others finished their preflight chores, wiped their hands, and lined up to greet the VIPs. A dozen well-dressed men and women, with their kids in tow, ambled over to the hangar.

Even VIPs could be impressed. They exclaimed the same

things—"Ooh," "Wow," "Cool"—that all the other parents and children said.

Jake had never seen any kind of celebrities. He wanted to get a glimpse of them. Hanging back behind the crew and pilots, shorter than everyone by at least a few inches, he couldn't see. He slid over to the side of the crowd and scanned the arrivals.

How disappointing—he didn't recognize any…oh shoot. Standing with a handsome man and a glamorous woman was Billy Grant.

As if Billy had radar, he swiveled his head and locked eyes with Jake. A slow, perfect smile dimpled his cheeks and showed off flawless teeth. "Jake Skyler," he said, like he was greeting a long-lost brother. "Come over here and meet my folks."

Mr. and Mrs. Grant turned from the pilots and looked Jake over, from his tattered sneakers to the glop of yellow paint that had dried in his hair. Billy's father tucked his hands deep in his pockets while Mrs. Grant hid hers behind her back. Jake didn't want to shake their hands anyway, but the insult caused a deep flush of embarrassment to burn his face and set his ears on fire.

Billy sauntered over and put his arm around Jake's shoulder. "Jake and I are in the same math class this year," he announced. "Isn't that wicked cool?"

"Charming," his mother murmured, giving Jake another once-over. Her hands came back around front, but now they rummaged in her purse, as if seeking self-defense. Maybe a can of Lysol. Or Raid.

"William," the father pronounced, "I believe it is time for your plane ride."

Billy patted Jake's back and then made a show of checking himself for wet paint. Jake couldn't understand what he'd done to deserve such cruelty.

Everyone's favorite sixth grader mimicked in his father's haughty New England accent: "Are you going to take a flight today, um, 'Jacob' is it?"

"It's just plain Jake."

"Oh, you're not so plain—you have some yellow highlights."

His mother laughed at that one, beaming at her son who continued in his regular super-cool voice, "Since you hang out here, I'll bet you get to fly all the time."

Nearby, Gabriel and Drew watched the interaction but neither one stepped in to correct Billy. Jake was grateful to the crewmembers, and he knew that his old self—Jake 1.0—would've spun big, elaborate lies about his flying adventures. But he wanted to be Jake 2.0, who told the truth and took his lumps and aimed to be Pilot in Command of his life.

He said, "I'm here to work, not have fun. The free plane rides are for the Young Eagles." After a pause, unable to resist, he added, "And sometimes little kids."

Billy's teeth snapped shut with a loud click. His parents shot

Jake a dirty look. Billy brushed back the sculpted hair falling over his perfect forehead and stalked off toward the planes. He grumbled, "Come on, let's get this over with."

After Billy had taken his flight with TC and paraded with his parents to their flashy SUV, the pilot—who looked unusually serious—quizzed Gabriel and Drew. The crew pointed him to Jake, who was cleaning his paintbrushes beside the outer hangar wall but watching the goings-on with great interest. Jake knew he'd made a bad impression on the VIPs. Maybe he'd gotten the Tiger Flight in trouble too. He stood and rehearsed his apology as he watched the pilot approach.

TC stepped up to Jake and adopted Winder's usual stance: arms folded, weight back on his heels. The sparkle had gone out of his eyes. He said, "That was the sourest boy I've ever taken up. I tried everything to make him laugh and enjoy himself, but he sulked the whole time." He narrowed his eyes at Jake. "Friend of yours?"

"No, sir. Just a guy in my math class."

"Did you say something that ticked him off?"

Jake inhaled. Here it comes, he thought. "I guess so. He was ragging on me so I defended myself."

TC nodded very slowly, like a judge who was making up his mind about a defendant's guilt. "I'd say you did a pretty good job," he replied. TC winked at him and strolled back to his plane.

Jake leaned against the hangar wall, weak with relief. He had dodged a bullet.

On Monday before the start of first period, however, Jake learned that the battle had just begun.

Adam dropped into his chair and bragged to one and all, "Man, that was a great time on Sunday. Wasn't it great, Peter?"

"Wicked cool," Peter said, unpeeling some paper from an expensive chocolate candy.

Adam snapped his fingers. "That's the word for it: wicked cool."

Glancing up from his laptop, Vic said, "That's two words, actually."

"What happened?" Jake couldn't stand the suspense any longer.

Adam, who was about to pummel Vic's computer, gave Jake an oh-you're-talking-to-me look of pretend surprise. Instead of answering, he organized his spiral notebook, pencil, and math book on his desk, something he'd never done before.

An expert at the silent treatment himself, Jake knew he could stand it. He thought about their comments just now and put it all together. With a glance toward the front of the classroom, where Perfect Boy was making Mrs. K laugh, Jake said in a soft voice, "I only know one other person who says 'wicked cool.' You spent Sunday with Billy Grant."

Adam switched his expression to a maybe/maybe-not pout.

Jake pointed at the treat that Peter savored with eye-rolling ecstasy. "He bribed you."

Vic turned his screen around to display a video game so hard to come by that parents were camping outside the stores to get one of the few copies. He said, "It wasn't a bribe. He wants to make new friends. I traded his dad some stock tips for this."

"Don't you see what's happening?" Jake slapped his desk in frustration. "He's using you to get back at me." He launched into the story of Billy and his parents' visit to the Tiger Flight hangar.

"I get it," Adam said. His tone became melodramatic. "We're just pawns in his evil game. There's no way he'd want to be friends with us. It's all about you."

On Jake's other side, Debra laughed. He whirled on her and said, "You think that's funny? Isn't this about the time you always butt in with something so smart it knocks us out of our chairs?"

She flushed and for a moment he thought he'd made her cry. Now he saw that Debra was mad. "It *is* funny," she said, though she sounded deadly serious. She had one of the expensive candies in her hand too. "You're so worried that everyone's against you, and you're so wrapped up in your obsession about planes and flying. If you had a little faith in your friends, you'd see that we miss you. We're just trying to make you realize that."

Adam nodded. "What she said." For once, he didn't dismiss her.

Peter said, “I second that.”

“Adam already seconded her,” Vic said. “You third her and I make it ‘unanimous,’ as my dad says.”

Jake was still looking at Debra. He asked, “You miss me?”

This time, he was sure he made her blush. She was sort of pretty when she wasn’t being such a pain.

CHAPTER ELEVEN

Three months into his worker responsibilities, on a gorgeous Saturday afternoon, Jake washed the second of the four planes, TC's N5464F. A gentle stream of water sluiced across the tiger-striped fuselage near the propeller. He'd helped his dad wash the family truck and car plenty of times, but those vehicles just drove around—these machines could *fly*. Doing that chore with his father had never felt this important, this respectful.

He rubbed the metal skin dry and stepped onto the black rectangle painted on the wing—the safety zone called the "wing walk"—to clean the canopy, which had captured a faint spray of droplets across the windshield. The water would evaporate and probably not leave a mark, but these planes were his responsibility. This was taking ownership. He told himself to follow through, to finish what he started. With a clean rag, he buffed the Plexiglas until he could see his reflection and that of someone standing behind him.

"Daydreaming?" Sunny asked.

"Uh, no, sir." Jake clambered off the wing, putting it between him and the pilot. He realized that for once he wasn't daydreaming at all—he was concentrating. He stammered, "I was, um, kind of caught up in my work."

Sunny nodded. "Yeah, we all noticed that you're really staying at it. Nose to the grindstone, shoulder to the wheel. You starting to love these flying machines?"

"Yes, sir. They're pretty special."

"And I'll bet you're still aching to go up."

"Absolutely positively." He told himself not to raise his hopes, but he couldn't stop the flutter building in his chest.

"Jake," Sunny said, "I think you've grabbed the dream."

Jake frowned. "Grabbed what?" What was he being accused of—stealing?

"The dream of flight. I mean, you're hooked—this place is your home away from home."

"It is. I love it here." He looked around at the hangar, the planes, the huge old Tiger Lady C-47. He hadn't put that feeling into words before, but he realized it was true.

He could still recall his initial jealousy and envy whenever one of the Young Eagles got to fly. Over time, though, he realized how privileged he was. Sure, he could only watch as kids his age took flight after flight, but working with the pilots and crew—and pampering those spectacular planes—now gave him a deeper appreciation of the skill and dedication of the Tiger Flight. For him, it was like the difference between getting invited on stage to participate in a magic trick and being the magician's assistant for the whole darn show. Grabbed the dream? Yeah, he held it tight in both fists.

Jake tried to explain it to Sunny, that feeling of certainty that he knew what he wanted to do when he grew up: to fly. "It all started when you guys flew over the hardware store in formation. Something, like, happened to me, inside me I mean…" There weren't good enough words—or he didn't know the right ones yet—to describe the feeling. Jake finally threw his hands up and said, "You had to be there."

"I was. I mean, I was leading the formation that day, so I was there with you. But I also felt what you're feeling when I was younger than you, maybe eight or so." Sunny came around the wing and leaned against the fuselage, arms and legs crossed, a far-off look on his face. "See, my dad took me to my first air show ever, where the Thunderbirds were performing. I remember there was a huge crowd with lots of grownups, and I was a little short for my age so I couldn't see a thing. It was killing me because I'd heard so much about the Thunderbirds. Now I was going to miss them, even though I was right there.

"Suddenly my dad points and says, 'Here they come.' I could hear their jet engines, but still couldn't see, so I did the most embarrassing thing for me, which was to ask my dad to pick me up. I thought I'd gotten too old for that. But he understood immediately and lifted me onto his shoulders. Now I was way taller than anybody else."

Sunny looked up to the sky as he relived the memory. "And there, just over the treetops came a flight of six planes toward me—the Thunderbirds, flying F-4E Phantoms. They were in their delta formation. From the ground they looked like a big white triangle as they headed my way. They must've been going 500 miles an hour, but I swear the whole thing happened in slow motion for me."

Jake said, "I believe you." In his mind he didn't see the famous Air Force jets, but instead he recalled the Tiger Flight soaring over Dad's hardware store in super slo-mo.

Sunny shook his head in wonderment. "It was the most beautiful thing I'd ever seen and then it got even better. Without warning, the six planes executed what the Thunderbirds call a 'bomb burst,' where they suddenly break formation in six different directions, like a firework exploding in the sky. Look!" He shoved up the sleeve of his flight suit and pointed at his forearm. "I've got goosebumps just telling you about it! I had goosebumps then too. I swear, I knew instantly, sitting on my dad's shoulders, I wanted to fly. I told him, 'That's what I'm gonna do.' And I meant it. Seeing myself flying those jets was the last thing I thought about when I went to sleep every night and the first thing when I woke up."

"I know about that too. Flying is all I think about, every

night and every day." Jake rubbed his cloth over the smooth, clean skin of the fuselage and asked, "Did you ever fly with the Thunderbirds?"

"Not as part of their team, but I've flown jet fighters. My dad had passed away by then, but it felt like he was there with me, you know? Anyway, I still go to sleep thinking about flying."

Jake said, "I'm gonna fly too. That's a no-brainer."

"Well," Sunny said, "I think it's time you experienced it firsthand and make sure you like it."

The cleaning rag fell from Jake's hands. "You mean I've paid off my debt?"

"Yeah, we agreed about that today, during debriefing. We'd like you to stay on as hangar kid if you want to—you'll do the same chores, but your reward will be to fly."

Jake snatched up the cloth and stuffed it in his back pocket. "Can we go up right now?"

"Into the wild blue yonder? That's why I'm here."

"Uh, all the Young Eagles have to bring a permission form signed by their mom or dad."

"I took care of it. I dropped by the hardware store at lunchtime and got your dad's signature. You're legal." He called to Drew and Gabriel, who had just finished wheeling two of the other planes into the hangar, "Hey guys, we're going up for a little turn in the air."

Gabriel swayed on his feet and Drew quickly steadied him.

Jake realized it was all an act—he was sure they knew about this. In mock wonder, Gabriel said, "You think little Jake can stand the excitement?"

Drew added, "You've never had anybody faint in your plane before."

"Settle down, you knuckleheads," Sunny said while the crew laughed. "Ready us for takeoff." He walked over to N5695F and waved for Jake to step up.

Jake climbed onto the wing and stepped onto the copilot seat. He sat carefully, as if afraid to wake himself from this dream. His hands clenched together, each holding the other one still, but his legs bounced up and down with adrenalin.

After showing Jake how to fasten the safety harness, Sunny brought up his forearms, stuck his thumbs sideways and motioned outward with each hand like he was hitching a ride in opposite directions. Drew, all business now, marched toward the plane, and Sunny then held both hands in the air to signal he wasn't touching anything.

Drew edged around the propeller, pulled away the orange chocks, and retreated. He placed the rope-linked wedges behind him and came to attention beside Gabriel.

Sunny shouted, "Clear!" and both crewmembers gave him a thumbs up. Sunny jabbed the starter button and the engine roared to life. The propeller spun so fast. Jake felt dizzy as he tried to follow the rotating blades, which blasted air backward into the cockpit. Sunny pulled the Plexiglas canopy closed over their heads. The noise level cut in half, and Jake pushed some windblown hair off his forehead.

Sunny said, "Put on your headset. The microphone is voice-activated, so move it close to your mouth."

The earpieces were cushioned and covered both sides of Jake's face; they immediately blocked out the rest of the engine sound. Then Sunny's voice came in loud through the headset speakers: "Can you hear me?"

"Yes, sir." Jake could barely hear his own voice—it sounded very far away. He pulled the foam microphone cover against his mouth and tried again: "Yes, sir." Now his excited voice sounded in the headset.

Sunny thumbed a button on the left-hand grip of the yoke. In an authoritative tone, he said, "Rome area traffic, November 5695 Foxtrot taxiing for Runway One, Rome."

In the silence that followed, Jake asked, "Are they supposed to answer?"

"Only if there's something I need to know about." He increased power by moving the throttle lever and pushed down the left rudder pedal. The pedal under Jake's left shoe moved inward too.

They turned to the left and cruised past Gabriel and Drew, who both saluted. Jake saluted back. The guys seemed genuinely pleased for him. Gone were the days when he was the punk who busted Sunny's wing.

Sunny taxied slowly—Jake knew he could bike faster than this. Then the pilot actually braked to a stop. He said through Jake's headset, "This is the run-up area, where we do our final check. With a physical checklist—" he pulled a laminated card from a niche beside the instrument panel "—and a mental one. First on the mental checklist, we always ask ourselves, 'Do I feel like flying?'" He grinned at Jake. "Well?"

"I do!"

"Me too." Sunny smiled even wider as he turned his attention to the checklist. He went over each item, reading it aloud and pointing to it on the instrument panel: "Altimeter set. Radios correct. Directional gyros set." When he came to the end, he slid the card back in place, locked the canopy on his left, and showed Jake how to fasten the clip on his side.

The pilot announced, "Rome area traffic, November 5695 Foxtrot taking Runway One and holding, Rome." He looked up through the canopy and around the plane, searching for hazards in the air and on the ground. Then he turned onto the runway and halted on the center line. He said, "Rome area traffic, November 5695 Foxtrot departing Runway One, eastbound departure, Rome."

Sunny increased the throttle and the engine revved faster and faster. His feet pressed both rudder pedals down together, which acted as a brake. The plane began to shake from the rising, pent-up power. He released the pedals and the twin-tailed tiger accelerated like a dragster finally getting the green light, pressing Jake back in his seat. Through his window, the concrete runway streamed past and lost focus. A rumble quaked through him as the plane went even faster. Jake's hands clutched his knees. Then all his weight fell into his shoes and his feet tingled and his stomach flip-flopped as the ground suddenly dropped away. He was flying!

Sunny pulled back on the yoke and the yoke in front of Jake rocked back too as the plane climbed fast. Jake's body felt almost weightless as the plane leveled off. Sunny said, "You doing okay?"

"Uh-huh. I mean, yes, sir."

"These Aircoupes don't do many aerobatics," he said. "I hope you won't be disappointed."

He turned sharply to the right. The plane rolled up on its left side and pulled through the turn, pressing Jake into his seat. For a couple of seconds he felt very heavy. Looking through his side of the canopy, he couldn't see the wing or any part of the aircraft. Spread below were fields and homes and the intersection of two roads, a big gray X two thousand feet beneath him. It felt like dream-flying, where he didn't need a plane—it was just him, the clouds, and the wild blue yonder.

Then Sunny leveled out and rolled the opposite way. Jake went from feeling as light as a feather to dense again. Now he watched Sunny looking down at the same unobstructed view he'd enjoyed seconds earlier. And he imagined himself in Sunny's seat, in control of the aircraft. A Pilot in Command.

When they flew level again, Sunny said, "Those are called banked turns. We took them at about 3 Gs—that's three times the pull of gravity. Neat, huh?"

"Yeah, I love it."

"Then are you ready for one of my personal favorites? Let me introduce you to Mr. Wingover."

Sunny climbed sharply—with nothing but blue sky for as far as Jake could see—and then turned hard, swinging around like a skateboarder reversing course at the top of the half-pipe. Green and brown fields, dotted with houses and sliced by roads, came into view as Jake's stomach somersaulted. Sunny flew them along that line for a few seconds, turned hard again and then once more, and climbed again. As Sunny guided them back toward their original position, Jake realized they'd made a figure 8 in the sky. That was too cool.

"Told you they were great fun," Sunny said, looking over.

Jake shook his head in amazement. His mouth hurt from smiling so wide.

Sunny leveled off and let the woods and grassy foothills leading to Lavender Mountain roll below them. From way up here they seemed to be the only ones left on Earth.

"Brace yourself," Sunny said. In one fluid motion, he

pushed in the left rudder pedal while turning the yoke to the left and reducing power. Jake's side of the plane rolled up as the left wing went down. Sunny held the turn steady as the plane flew ever lower in a tight, corkscrewing spiral. Lying on his side, Jake saw the world go around and around, like he was on a ship caught in a whirlpool—except no ship's captain ever smiled as broadly as Sunny. The pilot was in full control and loving it. Who said being in a "downward spiral" couldn't be fun?

Sunny pulled back slightly on the yoke and eased it to the right as he pushed in the right rudder pedal. Suddenly they pulled out of the spiral and were flying level again, leaving Jake lightheaded and giddy.

"Maaaaaaan, I love to fly," Sunny shouted, sounding as happy as a boy on the first day of summer vacation. Now only a few hundred feet above the ground, they appeared to be flying faster than ever, with trees whipping past beneath them at a dizzying rate. When Jake pointed this out, Sunny explained that it was an illusion: since the trees and other points of reference were closer, they only seemed to be going by faster than when the plane was up high.

Sunny pulled back on the yoke, applied power, and took them up to 2,000 feet above sea level. He asked, "Want to take over?" He glanced at Jake again.

"Yes, sir!" Jake curled his fingers around the soft rubber grips of the yoke. The power of the engine, the heartbeat of the tiger, surged through his hands and up his arms. There was another pulse-like rhythm too, the push of air against the wings and fuselage as the aircraft clawed its way through the sky. He held the plane steady, sure of himself and at ease. Flying was totally natural. It felt right.

As if reading his mind, Sunny said, “You look really comfortable, what we call wired into the plane. You think you might like to learn how to do this thing called flying?”

“It’s all I want to do from now on.” Jake experimented with tiny movements of the yoke, taking them a little higher and then lower.

“Then it’s time you plot your future and set some goals.”

Far below, Jake saw the airport and, beyond it across the highway, his father’s hardware store. *Sorry, Dad, the family business isn’t for me.* Jake knew exactly what he planned to do—who he wanted to be—when he grew up. At last he could answer his father’s question.

CHAPTER TWELVE

When Sunny taxied them back to the hangar, a feeling of letdown weighed on Jake as much as pulling three Gs. Now he knew how the Young Eagles felt and what da Vinci truly meant. The thought that he'd have to wait another week—or even longer—to go up again was the worst frustration he'd ever endured.

Through the headset, Sunny said, "Buck up, kid. Take a look out there."

Fury, Winder, Bones, and TC stood beside Drew and Gabriel, all of them signaling Sunny closer, arms moving back with perfect synchronicity. Jake's heart jumped into his throat. They were all waiting for him.

Sunny stopped and cut the engine. He gave Jake a huge smile before sliding the canopy back. Jake popped up alongside him as the small crowd burst into applause. Legs trembling with emotion, he stepped off the wing. The first ones to greet him were Gabriel and Drew with high fives and low fives and shimmy-shakes.

TC clapped Jake on the back. He said, "Your mom will be here shortly. Come up to the Pilots Lounge and we'll buy you a soda."

Gabriel said, "We gotta split. See you soon, hangar kid." He and Drew waved to everyone and set off toward the parking lot.

Jake followed the pilots into the hangar and upstairs to the lounge. Winder and TC sat at one table, Bones relaxed at another, and Fury straddled his chair at a third, Styrofoam cups of coffee or half-consumed cans of soft drink in front of them all.

Bones said, "How do you feel about your promotion, hangar kid?"

"Pretty good, Major," Jake said. "I'll never step on a plane the wrong way again."

TC said, "I'll drink to that," and everyone raised their cups and cans and took a gulp.

Sunny grabbed two colas from the fridge and handed one to Jake before pulling up a chair beside Bones. He said to the pilots, "I started telling Jake about setting goals."

"Easy to set 'em," Fury said. "Sometimes a challenge to keep 'em."

Winder leaned back against his chair and folded his arms, saying, "That's because people don't know how to do it right."

Sunny told Jake to grab a seat. Jake noticed one or more

available chairs at each table and hesitated about where to sit. It felt like picking sides in a game.

Fury said, "Hey, chief, sit down before you fall down." He put the sole of his boot against a chair close to him and gave it a shove. The chair skidded up to Jake, who stopped it, spun it around, and straddled the seat like Fury did, arms crossed over the top. From there, he could see everybody and he didn't have to show favorites. Perfect solution. He opened his icy cola and took a long swallow, feeling like one of the guys.

Sunny said, "Winder's right. The problem with setting a goal is people sabotage it right off the bat. They set themselves up to fail. Here's the thing—"

"Jake?" Mom's voice echoed from inside the hangar.

Jake looked at his watch. Shoot, it was 4:30. Just when he had settled in with his heroes.

TC trotted to the exit and called down, "We're all in here, Susan, torturing Jake with our alleged wisdom. Come on up."

Jake considered whether going home would be better than sitting there with his mother embarrassing him.

Mom's shoes clacked up the wood stairs. Even in her faded jeans and a casual shirt, she looked like the take-charge executive, the ruler of ten galaxies. So it surprised him when she hesitated in the doorway. She said, "I don't know. This looks like a boys' club to me."

Jake took a long slurp of cola to show that he agreed. No

girls allowed—see ya in the car.

Sunny said, "Actually I was stalling until you got here. We were just talking about Jake's future—he's going to need your help."

Jake gagged, almost spraying cola across the floor. Thank goodness he wasn't sitting with anybody.

Mom hesitated, as if wondering where the conversation was headed. She said, "Uh, that's an important thing to do. I can't remember Nick or I ever talking about goal setting." She paused again before cautiously asking, "What goal does Jake have in mind?"

"He wants—"

Winder interrupted Sunny. "We're really talking about setting any goal. It doesn't matter if Jake wants to be the best hangar kid on Earth, or get the best grades in school or become a teacher or an engineer or a doctor." He looked at Bones, who seemed to pick up some telepathic message from the again-silent cowboy.

"That's right," the doctor-pilot-soldier said. "If we've had any success in life, it's because we did a good job of setting goals for ourselves and following a plan."

Mom took a seat at the last unoccupied table, and Sunny fetched a soft drink for her. It was very weird to see her in the Pilots Lounge with all the guys, but now she didn't seem to mind being the only woman. Maybe she was used to it from working with a bunch of men at her office. Jake recognized her look of interest and concentration, the same expression he saw on Parents Night at school while she and Dad talked to Jake's teachers. She was into the conversation big time.

She said, "Okay, tell us how to do that, and Nick and I will make sure Jake follows through."

Sunny said, "It all starts with grabbing that dream, which Jake did. He had an exciting afternoon. He went up with me and—"

"Went up?" Mom's hand clamped around the soft drink can and squeezed, her knuckles so white that Jake flinched. Soon there would be soda everywhere. Winder, Bones, and TC shook their heads at Sunny while Mom growled, "You said he was on probation."

Fury jumped in. "It was my fault, Susan. Jake's been doing such a great job that I decided he needed a reward. All the guys agreed. We declared his debt paid in full and promoted him."

"So you took him flying," Mom said, her temper rising, "without my permission?"

Sunny said, "Um, actually I got Nick's permission today at the hardware store." Mom glared at him and Sunny began talking faster. "Once I told him Jake was out of hot water, Nick wanted him to be able to fly with us—so he signed the form."

"Then I'll take this up with him." Mom stood. "Come on, Jake. We'll go home and wait for your father." She stomped out and took the stairs with a hard, uncompromising stride.

The pilots all seemed to be shocked by the sudden turn of events. No one said a word.

Jake pushed out of his chair and stood at attention, looking at the stunned men. "Thanks for everything," he said in a mournful voice. Before he could see their reactions, he turned and fled from the room.

Mom drove Jake home in wounded silence as he tried to explain how it felt when he grabbed his dream. He failed even worse than he had with Sunny. At least Sunny knew exactly what he meant. For all Jake knew, the only dream his mom ever had was to make his life miserable.

Her car sailed into the open garage. Jake held his breath as she screeched to a halt, the front bumper only a few inches from the wall. She jabbed the button on the visor to close the overhead door.

Jake watched her march into the kitchen. He decided to stay in the car for a while. Funny, a couple of months ago he would've reacted to something like this by losing himself in his video game, but the last thing he wanted to do now was shoot some stupid squids. Mostly he wanted to think, to figure out what had gone wrong and how to make it right.

He sighed and unlatched his seatbelt. Jake 2.0 wasn't ever going to get a high score in anything fun—only in raising his parents' blood pressure. And here he was trying to be grown up and responsible and all the things Mom and Dad were always talking about.

Mom appeared in the doorway, hands on hips. "Well?" She shouted it so loud, the closed car barely dampened her volume. "How can we talk about this if you're hiding in there?"

"I wasn't hiding." He opened his door, got out, and thought about slamming it like she had done, but that would only make her madder. He pushed it shut and stalked toward her. "And a minute ago, you weren't talking."

She must've seen the righteous hurt in his face because she took a deep breath and dropped into a chair at the kitchen table. He closed the door and leaned against it. "Sit," she said. "I won't bite."

In the car, that's exactly what it looked like she wanted to do. Now he saw how tired her always-sad eyes were, how her shoulders slumped. The imperial queen during a bad turn in her reign. He sat beside her, his anger quickly draining away too. Tears pooled in her eyes and she whispered, "I worry about you. I have since you were born. Even before then, when I was carrying you."

"Why?"

"It's a mother's right."

"Well, you should be worried, driving me home the way you did."

Mom snorted and wiped her eyes. "You're right. No one should ever drive angry. I have to keep us safe, and also make sure I don't hurt anyone else."

"Kind of like a Pilot in Command."

"What's that?"

Jake was glad she sounded interested. Maybe this was the break he needed to change her mind. "Sunny says we have to answer for our choices. A Pilot in Command is responsible not only for his flight but for the people on the ground too."

Mom looked at him for a long moment and then started to cry again, her jaw quivering. Not the reaction he wanted. She settled down, and now her voice sounded firm, unyielding. "I'm sorry I behaved that way," she said, "to Sunny and the others. They're good men and they sound very wise. Now that you've paid your debt to them, I just want you to find other interests."

"What if flying is all I want to do?"

"Jake, I swear to—" She clenched her fists. "No. My word is final. You'll get over this. Remember how bad you wanted to be a pirate after that movie came out? You cried like a baby when we told you that was never going to happen."

"That was make-believe. I can really learn to fly. The Tiger Flight will teach me how."

"When you're eighteen, you can do what you want. For the next six years, though, I still make the rules."

Jake muttered, "Dad signed that form. He wants me to fly." He sent out a silent apology, asking his father's forgiveness for bringing up that sore point—only Dad could rescue his dream now, and Jake couldn't afford to play nice.

Mom shot him a furious look. "We'll see about that." She plucked the cordless phone off the wall and called Dad at the store. Though Jake could only hear her half of the conversation, he could tell his father was on the defensive.

Leveling an icy voice into the handset, Mom said, "Oh, sure you were getting around to telling me. You know how I feel about— Well, now you do."

She switched off the phone and dropped it onto the recharger stand. "That's the end of it," she told Jake. "I don't want to hear another word about planes or flying or pilots."

At dinner, Dad picked at his food and wouldn't look at anyone. He pushed chicken nuggets around on his plate with what Jake thought was mere random restlessness. Then he noticed that his father moved them in patterns before returning them to their original spots, the way he practiced chess moves. Dad was strategizing. Finally, he set down his fork and said, "Susan, we aren't done with this business of flying."

Mom, who had chopped each of her nuggets into four pieces and methodically snapped them up one by one, replied, "I am. Case closed."

Dad motioned to Jake, telling her, "I think he should tell us why he wants to fly."

"No," Mom said, "we went through this already. When he's eighteen, he can tell us off and fly to the freaking moon if he wants, but until then he doesn't get a say."

"He's not our prisoner," Dad said, still trying to sound reasonable. "You don't have to listen, but he has a right to talk. So, Jake, why do you want to fly?"

Jake had hoped Dad would do the hard work for him, but it made sense he'd have to defend himself. Maybe that's what his father had figured out working through the chess moves.

The imperial queen, the most powerful and dangerous piece on the chessboard, sat across from Jake. She stared over his head, as if waiting for him to get this over with so she could say, "No," and tell him to wash the dishes.

He took a drink of milk, decided on what he wanted to say, and began. "Every time I pushed a broom around the Tiger Flight hangar I kept reading this plaque that all the pilots signed. There's a quote on it from Leonardo da Vinci. It goes, 'For once you have tasted flight, you will forever walk the Earth with your eyes turned skyward, for there you have been and there you long to return.' That's the way I feel, okay?"

Dad nodded but Mom looked unmoved. So much for Leonardo.

Jake swallowed some more milk for courage and tried

his own words. "When the Tiger Flight flew over me that day behind Dad's store, something happened inside. I changed. Dad asked me that morning what I wanted to do when I grew up and I really didn't have a clue. Now I know." Mom began to shake her head, but Jake focused on what he had to say. "I want to make you all proud of me. I want to learn and get good grades and do something important. Maybe I can fly for an airline and keep hundreds of people safe at a time. Maybe I can fly military jets and protect America and folks around the world. Maybe I can fly in the Young Eagles Program and show kids like me how awesome the world is at 2,000 feet."

He took another drink and wiped his mouth on his napkin. "I'm gonna do one of those things, or maybe all of them like some of the Tiger Flight guys. And I'm not saying this stuff to hurt your feelings—I'm only telling you how it is. So here's the deal: I can miss out on six years of learning how to fly safe and smart from great pilots just up the road, and then hope that whoever shows me how to fly knows what he's doing. Or I can keep working for the Tiger Flight and pay attention to everything they teach me. I can learn to be a Pilot in Command. Not just in command of a plane, but in command of my life.

"If you were in my place, Mom," he concluded, "what would you want to do?"

CHAPTER THIRTEEN

On Sunday after lunch, Dad followed behind in the truck while Jake rode with his mom to the parking lot near the Tiger Flight hangar. The wind had picked up since morning and the skies threatened a downpour.

TC kneeled on the wing of his plane and was fooling with something in the cockpit. He looked up and waved to Jake and his parents as they walked over. Jake gave him a thumbs up and a big grin. The pilot pumped his fist and yelled, "Awright!"

His shout got the attention of the other pilots. They emerged from the hangar where two of the planes were sheltered and called their greetings, except for Winder who folded his arms, cocked his head to one side, and nodded. The laconic cowboy let a small smile crease his face.

Sunny greeted Jake's mom and dad. He looked like he was holding back a dozen questions.

Dad peered at the darkening clouds. The wind tousled his hair. "You going up today?"

"No," Fury said, joining them. "The winds are gusting to twenty knots, which is no fun, and rain is on the way. We had to turn away some Young Eagles, and we sent the crew home."

Jake's mom looked relieved. He knew she couldn't help it. To her credit, though, she didn't say anything.

Fat drops of rain smacked the pavement and the tops of their heads. Dad said, "I need to open up the store. See you soon!" He bopped Jake's shoulder affectionately and jogged back toward the truck.

Bones said, "Come inside. We've got coffee in the lounge."

Everyone quick-stepped under cover except Fury and TC, who had to retrieve their planes. While Fury placed a long, two-pronged fork around the front wheel of N5642F and effortlessly hauled the tiger-striped plane inside as if he was pulling a wagonload of kittens, TC made a hilarious show of fighting the wind while trying to tug his plane to shelter. Just as he rolled it into the hangar, the downpour started. Rain bounced high as it struck the concrete, and it beat the tall, peaked roof with hundreds of hammer taps. "Coffee," TC announced and led the charge up to the Pilots Lounge.

They settled in with steaming mugs, and hot cocoa for Jake. The pilots all sat where they had the day before, TC and Winder at one table, Fury in his backward chair at another, and Sunny and Bones at a third. Jake's mom sat at the last table, and this time he sat with her.

Sunny said, "Susan, we're so glad that you came back."

Bones raised his coffee cup. "Here, here," he said and took a drink of coffee. The others followed his lead. It reminded Jake of the gathering yesterday before the mood had turned sour. He caught himself hoping that his mom would keep her promise and stay cool. Have faith, he thought. She'd promised to have faith in him—he needed to show the same in her.

Mom dipped her head, her face coloring, as she said, "I want to apologize for my behavior yesterday." She looked up and made eye contact with each of the pilots as she continued, "I have to admit that I'll still worry about Jake—a mother never stops worrying—but since he's determined to learn to fly and follow in your footsteps, or maybe *contrails* is the better word, I hope you'll take care of him like he's your own son." Her eyes became teary. Mom breathed deeply and her voice grew strong again, almost icy now. She said, "He's the only one I have. I can't keep him locked away from the world. I know that."

"We understand," Sunny affirmed and the others echoed him. "But Jake's got a lot to learn before he actually flies a plane."

She took a drink of black coffee and shifted gears. "Okay," she said, "before I lost my cool on Saturday you were telling us about how to set goals."

Sunny responded, "What we were saying yesterday is that people fail to meet their goals because they don't do a good job of setting them. They don't understand all the ingredients involved."

He handed off the speech to TC, who said, “Here are the ingredients: take two eggs, a cup of milk—” Bones thwacked TC’s arm with his Tiger Flight ball cap and the jolly pilot started again. “Seriously, the first thing Jake needs is what he’s already got, which is his dream. He grabbed it; it’s his. In piloting terms, his dream is the fuel that’ll keep him moving toward his goal.”

Jake frowned, trying to keep it all straight: dream, fuel, goal. Fury waved to get his attention and said, “Look, chief, you can make up your mind you’re going to fly, but to do that you’re going to have to understand geometry and calculus and physics and much more. You’re sure to have times when you’re struggling with math, or whatever, and maybe you’ll think about quitting—that’s when your dream will give you the boost you need to keep going. You’ll think about not making it, not flying, and that’ll hurt so bad that you’ll push on through.”

“Okay,” Jake said. “I got it.”

Winder drank some coffee and tipped his black Tiger Flight cap farther back on his head as if it was a Stetson shading his eyes too much. “Next,” he said, “you need to understand what it takes to accomplish your goal and put together a plan to accomplish it. For flying, that’s where we come in. We’ll tell you what and how to study and practice.” He looked at the others, like maybe he’d used up his ration of words, but they motioned for him to keep going. He shrugged and continued, “What I said yesterday was that smart goal setting applies to whatever you want to do. Say you want to play quarterback on your middle school football team. Well, the best approach is to talk to coaches and players about what it takes to achieve that. You need to understand what you have to do to reach your goal—and that becomes your plan of action." He closed his mouth and leaned back, arms folded, done with talking.

"There are three kinds of people," Sunny said. "Those who make it happen, those who watch it happen, and those who wonder what happened." He pointed at Jake. "Which one do you want to be?"

"I'm gonna make it happen."

Sunny gave him a nod. "That's good. But even with your dream fueling you and knowing what you'll have to do, you still might fail unless you set a deadline—the date when you want to accomplish your goal."

"Without a deadline," Bones said, "you won't have any pressure on you to do anything. You can keep putting it off and say you'll get around to it whenever. And you never will." He sipped his coffee and went on, "It's also critical that you write all of this down: your goal, your plan, and the date when you're going to achieve your goal. Writing it down makes it real—it shows your commitment. Even better, find pictures of your dream and keep them in front of you. Put them on your walls, the mirror in your bathroom, on your notebooks, everywhere. They'll remind you of why you're working so hard."

Fury said, "The other thing people forget is maybe the most important detail: a reward for accomplishing your goal. When you succeed, you need to treat yourself to something."

TC nodded to Jake's mom. "Or get a reward from your parents—your mom would love to buy you a big, expensive present."

"Gee, thanks," Mom said and the others laughed.

TC grinned mischievously. "Really! A reward reinforces your dream. It makes all your hard work worthwhile. Even though we've been flying twenty years or more, the greatest reward was getting our wings, becoming a pilot. For all of us, that was one of the proudest moments of our lives."

Jake imagined having his own patch with silver aviator wings one day. He'd never wanted anything so desperately. "See if I got this right," he said, and counted off the goal-setting elements on his fingers. "Grab a dream, which becomes my fuel to get me to the goal. Set a date to finish my goal. Know what it takes to do the job, write it all down, and follow that plan. And, when I meet my goal by the deadline, give myself or *get*—" he smiled at Mom "—a reward."

She raised her coffee cup to him. "A-plus. I should've been using this stuff at the office years ago. We can use it on your schoolwork too."

"Since my dream is to fly," Jake agreed, "I need to do good in math."

"Do *well* in math," Mom corrected.

Bones said, "English is important too—though you can't tell that from listening to us."

Jake rolled his eyes. "Whatever. Anyway, let's say I want to get a perfect score on my math homework that's due tomorrow." He asked his mother for a piece of paper and a pen, and he started writing as he spoke. "I have my dream of flying and my homework goal. Mrs. K told me what I need to study and what problems to practice, so my plan is to do that. And now I set a deadline—today at 6 o'clock—and if I get 100 on it…I want a sports car." He raised his arms in triumph. "Fab-u!"

Fury shook his head. "Sorry, chief. The reward's too big for such a tiny goal. They should be the same size. You get a sports car for scoring an A on sixth-grade math homework, how're you going to celebrate when you get your wings? Buy an island in the South Pacific?"

Jake pouted as he scratched out his sports car reward. "Man, you're harsh."

Mom said, "How's this: I'll take you and your dad out for ice cream if you get a perfect score."

"That's okay, I guess." Jake wrote it down. Then he said, "Wait a sec. Why does Dad get a reward too?"

Mom grimaced and looked away. She murmured, "I owe it to him."

Sunny said gently, "You owe it to yourself too. You haven't had an easy weekend."

"Yeah," she said, "I guess Nick and I have a lot riding on Jake achieving his goal."

CHAPTER FOURTEEN

"You got a hundred?" Adam said, looking from his graded homework to the paper Mrs. Kirby just handed to Jake. "No way. What'd you do, take a smart pill?" Even months later, with school almost over, he was still sore about not being able to go over to Jake's house on Sundays. If anything, the extra time at his own house had worsened his grades.

Vic said, "We should dust it for fingerprints and then compare it with his mom and dad's. Maybe look for DNA traces in case one of them sneezed on it." Before Adam could punch him, he swiveled around and inserted his B-plus homework into his portable three-hole punch, set the page in a binder, and clicked the rings shut. Then he opened his laptop and entered his score into a spreadsheet, which updated the graph he'd started last August.

Jake stared at the grade at the top of his paper, 100 in a big circle with "Nice job!" and a smiley face written beside it. He'd never seen such a grade so close to his name before.

Debra, of course, got them all the time. Jake cut his eyes her way, trying to be smooth about it, and sure enough there was yet another perfect score on her paper. But that was all, just a grade. He looked down his nose at her. "No 'Nice job'? No smiley?"

She sniffed back, "Mrs. Kirby only does that when a miracle occurs."

All of Jake's buds, even Adam, cracked up. Mrs. Kirby swung her laser-beam eyes at them, which produced instant silence.

Jake mumbled, "It really worked."

"What," Adam said, "you find a genie in a bottle?"

"I wrote down my goal and a plan and a deadline, I studied and did the work, and…I won."

Peter gulped down a whole peanut butter cup and wiped his fingers on his C-minus homework. He asked, "What'd you win?"

"My mom's taking me out for ice cream."

"No kidding?" Peter took out his seldom-used notebook and a pencil, which was still like new even though it was May. "Okay, dude," he said, "run through those steps one more time."

With Mom's permission, the men of the Tiger Flight started to give Jake short lessons in piloting. Jake adopted the uniform worn by the crew—black tee and olive drab pants—but being just a hangar kid he didn't merit a name badge or the coveted

Tiger Flight patch yet. The pilots were also very strict about when they let him in the planes; he first had to finish all the jobs they gave him, and do them well.

Thanks to the goal-setting lessons, he set his sights on the reward they offered, paid attention to his deadlines, and worked hard at his plan. Thus, every weekend, after the last of the Young Eagles had flown, he got to sit in the copilot seat of one of the tigers, and learn about the instrumentation, how to use the radio and change frequencies, and—the most exciting—how to taxi the plane up and down the tarmac. According to the plan he'd written down, he wanted to graduate from taxiing to learning to fly by his thirteenth birthday in August.

Jake wouldn't be able to get his learner's permit to drive a car for three more years, so it thrilled him that he could practice taxiing a plane. He'd figured that guiding the plane along the tarmac would be like driving a car, but the process was completely different. Despite the appearance of the yoke, with its left- and right-hand grips, it wasn't a steering wheel; the pedals on the floor actually moved the plane left and right, and pushing them down together braked the aircraft. The yoke was used only for flight controls, moving the plane up and down while in the air. Although he wouldn't experience that until August, he knew he'd get there by the date he set—his plan said so.

"That's it," Bones said, resting his feet on the pedals, which moved under him as Jake maneuvered the plane to a stop in front of the hangar. "You're developing a nice touch, smooth as a surgeon's."

Jake asked, "Can I go up and back one more time?"

"Better power down. The guys want to talk to you about something."

"Uh oh." Jake followed the shutdown checklist for the engine and watched the spinning propeller slow to a halt across his half of the windshield. He lifted the headset from his ears and looked at Bones.

The pilot's eyes were masked behind sunglasses and his smooth face gave away nothing. As usual, his bulldog body moved with forceful efficiency. He reached up to the middle portion of the canopy and pushed it back. With two quick hops, he went from being seated to standing on the wing.

Jake deplaned with much more effort, partly due to distraction. His back and feet continued to tingle from the remembered rhythm of the engine, and his ears stayed warm long after he'd taken off the headset. Since the piloting lessons started, he could recall those same sensations whenever he was drifting off to sleep or waking up. He couldn't think of the last time he'd wanted to switch on his handheld video game, but he knew every day he wanted to fly.

He wondered if the pilots had decided not to give him lessons anymore. Was that the last time he'd sit in the copilot seat?

Bones led him up to the Pilots Lounge. Winder had left earlier to captain a commercial flight to Mexico, but Fury, TC, Sunny, and the crew had gathered at the tables there.

TC was finishing a story: "…and that's when I remembered where I'd left my wingman."

The other guys laughed, and Jake hoped he'd retell it from the start, but everyone turned serious when they saw him and Bones at the doorway.

In a low, melodramatic tone, Drew hummed the *Dragnet* theme: "Hmmm-hm-hm-hm."

Gabriel shielded his face, either to hide a smile or so he wouldn't have to witness Jake's impending doom. Jake was sure he'd know which one it was soon enough. He chose Fury's table and swung his chair around backward the way the big man sat.

Sunny said, "School almost over?"

"Yes, sir."

TC asked, "How are your grades?"

"Much better since you taught me about goal setting and following a plan. I showed my buds how to do it and they're getting higher scores too." Adam had been the final holdout, but even he'd tried it for the latest test and nailed his first B in sixth grade. Too bad he'd waited until the end of the school year.

Sunny picked up the conversation again. "Well, Angel and Drew here are taking finals and they have to study next weekend. Unfortunately, that's when we're doing our first air show of the year, on the other side of Atlanta. Normally the crew flies in with us and makes sure no one touches the planes all weekend." He tapped his fingers on the table, drawing out the suspense. "You think your parents would let you serve as the Tiger Flight crew for this show?"

"They better!" Jake exclaimed. "I mean, yeah, I think they'll be cool with it."

He wanted to call his mom—well, maybe his dad first—and ask permission, but then he reconsidered. Having the pilots ask for him was the smarter way to go. They knew all about those shows and could answer any questions Mom or Dad would have. He said, "Can you ask my mom when she gets here?"

Fury said, "That's the plan, chief. If she gives us the thumbs up, Gabriel and Drew will tell you what you need to do at the show, how to talk to the people there—be polite but commanding—all that stuff."

"Will I get to wear the patch?" Jake pointed at the yellow-bordered Tiger Flight shield over the right side of Gabriel and Drew's shirts.

Bones said, "We'll see. These guys work hard for that privilege, so we don't give out those things lightly."

TC leaned forward and said, "But tell you what—if you keep your grades up in school, stay on top of your hangar kid chores, study the aircraft manuals we give you, and practice the cockpit lessons, you'll earn your patch. Deal?"

The echo of heels on concrete sounded inside the hangar. Mom called up to them, "Is the lounge open?"

Jake told TC, "It's a deal." He ran to the door and waved her up. "Hurry, Mom. The guys have something to ask you."

His mother paused, her expression hardening. Then she seemed to give herself a talking to. She squared her shoulders and walked up the stairs to the lounge. From the doorway, she said, "Every time I come up here, something big happens."

"It's that time again," Sunny said. "Please have a seat."

CHAPTER FIFTEEN

The following Saturday, with a thin mist swirling across the highway just after sunrise, Jake sat in the family pickup truck beside Dad. They were headed to the Tiger Flight hangar. The plan called for Jake's father to drop him off and then drive the sixty miles to the air show, while Jake flew there on tiger-striped wings. They had a free motel room for Saturday night, complements of the sponsors of the show, and, after another day of displaying the planes, would get home to Mom on Sunday evening.

Jake figured he could make the journey to the show in less than half the time it took Dad: there were no speed limits or stoplights in the wild blue yonder. He wondered if pilots got seriously frustrated in traffic jams, knowing they could fly over everything and everyone if only they had wings and a rudder.

He looked forward to the weekend. Gabriel and Drew had briefed him on proper etiquette when dealing with the public, the typical questions he could expect about flying and the Tiger

Flight, and safety around the aircraft. They even called the house a couple of times during the week to quiz him. He was ready. Too bad Mom decided not to come along—she would've been proud when she saw him in action.

Jake asked his dad, "You're absolutely positive Mom won't go?"

"Sorry, partner, your mama is positively absolute about staying home." His expression became serious. "I used up my last bit of goodwill just getting her okay for *you* to go. And I had to go into big-time goodwill debt so you could fly there." Dad turned onto the airport access road, the truck headlights cutting through the fog. He said, "Remind me to tell you about emotional bank accounts sometime. It's even worse to overdraw one of those than the kind with money in them."

"What's up with her anyway? You should see the Young Eagles' parents—they can hardly wait for their kids to fly—but Mom's all doom and gloom."

"That's her business," Dad said. "When it's the right time, she'll tell you."

"Oh man, 'the right time' speech again."

"Hey, she didn't even tell me until I got in her doghouse by signing that permission form."

"Is it something bad?"

He opened his mouth, closed it, and then said, "Nice try."

"If she came to the air show, she'd see the way everyone

loves the pilots and gets so excited by the planes. Then maybe she'd be on my side too."

"She's not against you." He yawned long and loud. "If she was, we'd still be sound asleep in our beds."

Not me, Jake thought. I'd be thinking about biking over here, sneaking in, and stowing away on one of the planes.

He knew better than to say that. Instead, he checked the pockets of his olive drab pants for the umpteenth time to make sure he had spending money, identification, and the list of family phone numbers his mom insisted he take. His feet kicked against a small duffle that held a second crewmember uniform of black tee and "OD" pants, plus clean underwear—two sets, at his mother's insistence.

At the airport vehicle gate, Dad punched in the security code and waited for the fence to slide aside. He drove them to the side of the Tiger Flight hangar where the pilots had parked their trucks and cars.

The gentle sunrise created a scene of soft light and mysterious shadows in the mist. Each plane and pilot was a silhouette surrounded by swirling golden air. It looked magical, but this was real magic, not some fantasy from a book.

Jake hated to spoil the image by walking into it. Fortunately, his father wasn't ready to let him go yet. Dad said, "Don't be too hard on your mom. She's trying to be excited for you, to let you do something that's important to you." From his shirt pocket, he removed a small object and handed it over.

Jake fingered the hard rectangle of plastic. A thin metal pin was clipped to one side; the other side felt smooth except for grooves cut into the surface. He asked, "What is it?"

Dad flicked on the dome light, and the sudden brightness caused Jake to squint. The windows now reflected the interior of the truck—beyond them, the shadowy forms and sunlit fog disappeared. He held a black nametag with "Jake Skyler" etched in white.

"It's a present," his father said. "Your mom thought everyone at the air show should know who you are."

"It's perfect." Jake studied the back, unclipped the bright brass pin, and attached the nametag through the left side of his black t-shirt. If the pilots let him wear the Tiger Flight patch, it would go on his right. Thanks to Mom, he'd look even more like an official crewmember.

He said, "Dad, what's an emotional bank account?"

"All of us have one with each other. When you do or say something nice, you make a deposit into your account with the other people. If you hurt them by doing or saying something they don't like—even if you didn't mean to hurt them—you make a withdrawal from that account. The bigger the hurt, the bigger the withdrawal." He pantomimed reading a piece of paper. "In their minds, they can look at the total of your account with them anytime they want. If they see that the balance is negative, meaning you've withdrawn too much, you're in their doghouse."

Jake thought about it, how he still was in Adam's doghouse, how he put other people into his own doghouse when they ticked him off. He asked, "Can you have too many deposits?"

"Never," Dad said. "It's smart to make deposits by doing and saying nice things as often as possible, because there are sure to be times when you mess up. It doesn't matter if you think you're right; if the other person thinks you're wrong, they count that as a withdrawal."

Jake said, "So you're in Mom's doghouse?" His dad nodded in response, and Jake replied, "Even though you've made lots and lots of deposits?"

Dad laughed through his nose, nodding again. "That's the funny thing about people. One hurtful thing can blow away a dozen—sometimes a hundred—nice things you've done. Think of making deposits as putting one or two coins on other people's tables each time. When you make a withdrawal, they can take away a handful of coins or, if what you did hurt them a lot, they can sweep their arm across the whole tabletop." He stared straight ahead, his somber expression reflected in the glass. "Believe me, one word or one deed can knock all your hard work onto the floor."

"So you hurt her because of me?"

"I didn't mean to, and I didn't want to, but I know what it

feels like to pursue a dream. And I think wanting to be a pilot is a great dream to go after. I stood up for you because I thought you needed some wind at your back, a little push to help you on your way."

Jake asked, "Am I in Mom's doghouse too?"

"Not anymore. That's what's great about being a kid: you never stay in your parents' doghouse for long. Do one nice thing and you're back in the game." He switched off the dome light and said, "See you in a few hours, partner."

"I'll be waiting for you," Jake teased. "I bet I'll beat you there by at least ninety minutes."

"You're on. The loser buys the first round of funnel cakes."

He put out his hand for Jake to shake it, but Jake slipped inside Dad's arm and gave him a big hug. Over his father's shoulder, he said, "Thanks for everything. You're the best dad ever."

Dad said, "I always thought so."

Jake was still smiling as he grabbed his duffle and stepped down from the truck. Hardly any drop to the ground at all. He felt as if he'd grown tall on the trip from home.

The sun had risen higher and the fog retreated, leaving the air warm and humid. Now he could see every detail of the twin-tailed tigers and the pilots about to tame them once again. Dad honked the horn twice, which prompted a goodbye wave from Winder, Sunny, TC, and Fury. Jake gave his father a thumbs up before the truck reversed and headed to the exit.

“Morning,” Jake called. “Who am I flying with?”

All of the pilots pointed at each other.

“You guys.” He tried to sound exasperated, but had to admit they could be pretty funny. Spending a whole weekend with them was going to be major-cool.

Fury climbed atop his wing and stood over Jake like a giant as he wiped dew from the Plexiglas canopy. He said, “We drew straws and I got the short one.”

Jake asked, “So you won?”

“No, chief, I lost. You’re flying with me.” He climbed down and took Jake’s duffle, looking stern. But then he winked and Jake laughed with relief. The big man slung the bag into the cargo hold behind the seats where his own military-style carryall lay.

Jake greeted the others on the way to the Ready Room for the preflight briefing. Each one took the seat with his name on it. Jake sat in the second row, in Bones’ chair; the doctor-pilot-soldier was teaching at a military hospital that week.

Winder led the briefing since he would be leading the flight. Standing at a tall metal podium, he reminded everyone about the private radio frequency they’d switch to after takeoff, reported the weather conditions they could expect, and described the maneuvers they would practice on the trip. He also detailed their arrival procedures. The other pilots took notes on a Tiger Flight Brief Sheet, and Jake found himself nodding along with them. His face took on their serious expression, the same frown of concentration.

"Any questions?" Winder asked. When no one replied, he called Jake to the front of the room. Jake was filled with so much excited anticipation, he had trouble walking up to the podium.

The lead pilot said, "In recognition of your hard work and the achievement of your goals to date, this weekend you get to wear the crewmember hat—" he took a black "Tiger Flight Crew" ball cap from the top of the podium and slid it on Jake's head "—and the Tiger Flight patch."

Jake could barely keep still as Winder showed him the cloth shield with its royal blue background, bright yellow border, and the winged, two-tailed tiger roaring over top of a streaking bolt of lightning. At the pointed bottom of the shield, in black stitching, were the words "Tiger Flight." He'd never wanted anything more. The pilots had just made a huge deposit in his emotional bank account—it felt like they'd backed up a dump truck filled with coins and opened the release gate.

On the back of the patch, Winder had glued a soft Velcro tab. He stuck a wiry piece of Velcro on the right side of Jake's shirt and pressed the patch into place. Then the pilot turned Jake by the shoulders so that he faced the others, who broke into applause.

"Okay," Winder said, "let's fly."

The pilots resumed their serious demeanor, what Jake

thought of as their "formation expression." They marched out to the planes as a team, not as individuals, with Jake trailing. He imagined a military band on the tarmac playing something patriotic for them and cheering crowds fluttering handkerchiefs and throwing paper streamers. He couldn't help raising his arms in triumph.

Each pilot did a final walk-around inspection of his plane. Jake followed Fury in a circle around N5642F, looking where the big man looked. During the week, Debra's uncle—the mechanic named Max—had changed the oil and replaced the brake pads on each of the aircraft and refueled them. Everything looked spotless in the bright morning sunshine thanks to Drew and Gabriel.

The pilots met in front of the hangar, closed and locked the doors, shook hands, and wished each other a good flight. While shaking Jake's hand, they all complimented him on the nametag his mother had designed and how well the crew cap and Tiger Flight patch suited him.

Jake followed Fury back to his plane, the fourth one in line. He knew to watch the big man for cues about what to do next as the formation team continued their preflight checks. Fury put his foot on the black rectangular wing walk and turned his head to watch Winder, who had his foot on the wing of Tiger 1. Jake imitated Fury. Looking down the row at Sunny poised on the next plane, TC ready to mount Tiger 2, and Winder looking back at them, he could feel the tension building inside him. He wanted to do everything with precision and correctness—to truly be part of the flight and not some tagalong.

Winder gave a thumbs up with his right hand and everyone instantly responded with the same. The lead pilot's intense gaze swept over every face, including Jake's. Winder nodded. Everyone hoisted themselves onto their wing and entered their cockpit.

Jake strapped himself in beside Fury, satisfied when his seatbelt clicked into place at the same instant the pilot's did. Fury plugged in his headset but left it on his lap, so Jake followed suit. Jake glanced to his right and saw that Sunny was looking in his direction. From watching the formation in practice, he knew that TC was watching Sunny as Winder focused on TC. Beside Jake, Fury gave an emphatic thumbs up. Sunny signaled TC in kind and the gesture was repeated to Winder, meaning that the whole flight was good to go. The action was as smooth and quick as a row of dominoes tipping over.

Winder twirled his finger like a mini tornado, the signal for everyone to prepare to start his engine. Fury yelled, "Clear," at the same time as the others, a whole deep-voiced chorus. Winder patted the top of the black Tiger Flight ball cap on his head, as if to say, "Watch me." He then gave an exaggerated head nod and Fury and the others pushed their starter buttons.

The four engines came to life as one and a cyclone of

propellers blew air back into the open canopies. Fury and the others closed their cockpits and put their headsets on for the radio check. Out of habit, Jake pulled the foam microphone cover to his mouth even though he knew better than to interrupt.

Winder's voice came through Jake's speakers: "Tiger Flight, check in."

"Tiger 2," TC said.

"Tiger 3," Sunny said.

Fury said, "Tiger 4."

"Rome area traffic," Winder announced, "Tiger Flight, four aircraft, taxiing for Runway One, Rome."

Jake felt his excitement rise. Goosebumps played across his arms and down his legs, which bounced against the seat. Winder turned his plane and paraded past the others up the taxiway. TC followed, then Sunny, and then Fury in Tiger 4, each maintaining the same spacing between planes.

After Winder announced to Rome area traffic that Tiger Flight was taking the runway and holding, TC drew alongside Winder. Sunny in Tiger 3 squared up behind the lead and Fury pulled behind Tiger 2. As they sat two by two at the end of the long strip of blacktop—where Navy pilots used to land their Corsairs in World War II—Winder looked at TC, TC looked diagonally over his left shoulder at Sunny, and Sunny turned his face toward Fury. Fury gave him a thumbs up and the signal zigzagged from Tiger 4 to 3 to 2 and back to 1.

"Rome area traffic," Winder proclaimed, "Tiger Flight, four aircraft, departing Runway One, Rome. Eastbound departure." He twirled his finger to TC and the signal passed all the way to Fury.

Holding his feet on the pedals, Fury throttled up to 2200 RPM. The plane shook, rattling Jake, as the engine seemed to cry out for release. Fury gave Sunny his thumbs up and again the action ricocheted to Tiger 1.

Winder patted his head and nodded. Immediately, he and TC released their brakes and rocketed down the runway, side by side. Jake sat tall in his seat, craning his neck so he could watch them as they got smaller and smaller ahead of him. From the briefing, he knew Sunny and Fury would wait six seconds before following. He forgot to count after "three Mississippi," though, because of the sheer beauty of Tiger 1 and Tiger 2 suddenly lifting off together, picture perfect. Soft sunlight bathed the orange and black wings and winked off the canopies as the planes rose higher.

Fury released his brakes as Sunny did the same. The force pushed Jake back into his seat—Tiger 4's power was finally unleashed. Looking past Fury, Jake watched Sunny's plane as Fury kept pace alongside. They thundered down the runway together. Then Jake's stomach flip-flopped when Fury pulled back the yoke and they took off in a graceful climb. Tiger 3 was airborne beside them. Fury flew off Sunny's wing as rock-solid steady as a granite shelf.

Jake had never flown in formation before, and the close-up view of the other three planes amazed him. They seemed as tightly grouped now as they did sitting on the airfield. Instead of flying in a line, though, they settled into the fingertip formation. Winder flew the farthest ahead. Slightly below him and back to his left, TC in Tiger 2 took up position. Sunny slid just below and behind Winder's right flank, and Fury maintained an identical spacing to Tiger 3. Maybe four feet separated one pilot's wing from another's.

Jake had witnessed their close formations from the ground, but had never imagined that someone could jump from one wing to another. The discipline they showed in preflight check now made sense: such precision and focus paid off in the air.

"Tiger Flight," Winder ordered, "go Tac One."

As briefed, each pilot checked in before the frequency change to acknowledge the order. Jake heard a crisp "Tiger 2," from TC, followed by Sunny's "Tiger 3," and then Fury stated, "Tiger 4."

Fury pushed the preset button on his radio to switch to the "tactical" frequency Winder stated at the briefing. Since few other pilots used it, the flight wouldn't have to deal with background chatter.

On the new frequency, Winder said, "Tiger Flight, check in."

"Tiger 2."

"Tiger 3."

Fury said, "Tiger 4." His face remained turned to the left, where Winder's head was visible above and beyond Sunny's plane. As on the ground, the lead communicated by hand signals as much as voice, and Jake saw that the other pilots focused solely on Winder as well. Only the lead watched the skies ahead and around the flight, protecting them as he guided the pilots to their destination. And Fury, Sunny, and TC would follow Winder wherever he went, because they keyed off the lead rather than what was happening in front of them. The leader shouldered an awesome responsibility.

"Pilot In Command." Jake heard his own voice through the speakers against his ears, instantly embarrassed that he'd spoken without Fury's permission. Fortunately, his microphone was set to only transmit inside Tiger 4.

The big man's mustache twitched with what Jake realized was a smile. Without turning his head, Fury said through Jake's headset, "You got it, chief. Someday you can be one too."

Jake relaxed; the pilot wasn't angry with him at all. "You think so?" Jake asked.

"Just like these planes you love so much, you were designed to succeed."

Fury's voice grew gentler, as if he was speaking to one of his children. "Built by the best," he said. "Destined to fly."

CHAPTER SIXTEEN

The Tiger Flight made a big entrance at the air show a half hour later. Winder led them in a diamond formation that streaked past the airfield, a thousand spectators gasping and cheering. Jake knew exactly what they saw. He could still recall every detail from the first time he'd witnessed the same thing, when he stood behind Dad's hardware store. But experiencing the flyby while sitting in Tiger 4—which was in the "slot" behind the lead aircraft, with a Tiger outside every cockpit window and the airfield zipping beneath at 120 miles per hour—was a gazillion times better.

Butterflies of excitement raced through Jake's chest as Fury's plane zoomed along behind the Winder. His feet felt heavy and tingly, while his head was as light as a balloon. An ache spread across his face from smiling so wide and for so long, but he couldn't help himself. It took all his willpower to keep from shouting at the thrill of it all.

He was still only the magician's assistant, mostly watching

things right along with the audience, but he had the best darn seat in the house.

Jake knew the experience must've wowed Fury too, but the pilot didn't let on. Every bit of him concentrated on watching the lead plane only a few feet ahead of his propeller and reacting as soon as Tiger 1 did anything, as if a steel rod connected their aircraft.

Such intense work and focus for so long had caused sweat to darken Fury's flight suit from the neck to his waist. If the perspiration bothered the big man, he didn't show it. His hands remained locked on the yoke. Confidence radiated from his face—the look of being "wired into the plane."

The pilot had become one with his aircraft. He was a part of it, and it was part of him.

Jake had never seen focus like this before. He wondered if the pilots were even aware of their own thoughts when they were in this zone. Flying only a few feet away from Tiger 3 on one side, Tiger 2 on the other, and Tiger 1 in front, a pilot could get into trouble daydreaming or getting distracted. Reflex and instinct had to keep everyone safe—no wonder they practiced so much.

Winder led the diamond formation around the edge of the field, showing the crowd their tiger-striped tops and twin tails, and then they shot by those on the other side of the airport. Jake imagined their wild cheers and applause, like the reaction to the New Year's Eve ball drop and a Fourth of July fireworks show all in one.

When the flight touched down and taxied in formation to the parking area, rows of spectators surged toward the yellow tape that separated them from the blacktop. People aimed their cameras at the twin-tailed tigers while others nudged their kids and pointed. The children waved and adults gave the pilots a thumbs up. Jake knew they were signaling their compliments to the men who'd flown the planes, but it felt like they'd come out to see him too.

After the Tiger Flight followed their engine shutdown procedure, Fury took off his sunglasses, tilted back his sweat-stained cap, and turned to Jake. The sheer joy in the man's shining face made Jake smile even broader. He knew he'd always remember that look of achievement and pride and happiness. It was the picture of someone who had followed his plan and achieved his goal, a person who was living his dream.

The thrill of that flight carried Jake through the long day. Glaring sunshine, heat, and humidity gave him a taste of the broiling summer to come. He patrolled around the tiger-striped aircraft, which the pilots had maneuvered into a tight diamond, and answered questions until he was hoarse. The crush of spectators wanting to see the planes had forced officials to ring the aircraft with yellow tape stretched between orange and white traffic barrels.

Parked all around the twin-tailed tigers were gleaming

jets, sleek as quicksilver, powerful as rockets, but their spokespeople stood in the shade of their fancy planes, hands in pockets, hardly anyone to talk to. The Tiger Flight attracted a lot of the attention.

Jake kept moving inside the ring. An unending stream of people asked questions, and he glided smoothly from group to group to answer them. The pilots had worked the early shift with him and had promised to return later to give him a break. After his initial nervousness disappeared, Jake didn't mind. He enjoyed pacing within the tape like a restless jungle cat.

The patch, nametag, and crew cap were badges of honor. Everyone identified him as being part of the Tiger Flight, and they all wanted to photograph him and hear how a twelve year old achieved such an important position. By lunchtime Jake had told the tale so often that he'd distilled it into a two-minute adventure story that seemed to satisfy adults and kids alike. The grownups shook his hand and wished him luck; the teens and kids high-fived him and told him how lucky he was.

He especially liked to talk to fellow middle-schoolers. They asked the usual questions about the planes and what it felt like to ride in one, but he usually managed to steer the conversation toward the lessons of the Tiger Flight pilots: You were designed to succeed. Grab a dream. Set a goal and follow your plan. Be the Pilot in Command of your life.

Dad came forward during a brief lull when the crowds went

in search of lunch. He carried Jake's second funnel cake of the day with extra powdered sugar. The first one had been to pay off his debt, since Jake had beaten him to the air show by almost two hours. He handed over the treat, along with a tall, fizzing cola, saying, "You earned it, buddy. I'm just so danged proud of you—you make me wish there was a Not-So-Young Eagles program for guys like me."

Jake puffed up with the compliment. He thanked his dad and held the plate of hot, sugary fried dough away from his body as he ate, mindful of his black shirt. In four long slurps, he finished off the cola. Nonstop talking had given him a powerful thirst.

Another group of kids and adults roamed over. Dad said, "I'll catch you later. Those pilots leaning against their fancy jets next door to you look lonely. I feel sorry for them." With a grin, he snapped some photos of Jake talking to the new batch of onlookers and strolled away.

"Hey, Jake!" a familiar voice shouted from the other side of the ring. Jake finished with his story and answers and quick-stepped over. Adam stood there gawking with Vic and Peter. They kept looking from Jake to the planes and back, as if to say, "What's wrong with this picture?"

Jake spread his arms and lifted his head to show off his uniform, the nametag, and—most importantly—Tiger Flight patch and crew cap.

Peter seemed to have forgotten all about the triple-scoop

ice cream cone dripping in his fist. He said, "Un-freaking-believable. I mean, you showed us the pictures and videos on their website, but…wow."

"Pretty cool, huh?" Jake stood at parade-rest, his hands behind his back and feet spread wide, beside the yellow-spiraled nose cone of the closest plane. "This is an Aircoupe, as the website explained. It's what they call a 'war bird,' meaning it's been used in military service. In World War II, the Army Air Forces, as it was called back then, used them as a test bed to develop jet-assisted takeoff technologies. They were also used to hunt submarines and—" He stared at Adam's look of concern. "What?"

Adam said, "'Jet-assisted takeoff technologies'? You're starting to sound like this guy." He elbowed Vic, who stood so much taller that the bony tip bounced off Victor's belt buckle. Adam cried, "Ow!"

Vic didn't seem to notice. He murmured, "Development test bed," and thumb-tapped notes into a microcomputer held in his interlaced fingers.

However, Jake's best bud wasn't through yet. Adam stepped over the yellow tape and mimicked Jake's stance near the propeller. Adam said, "What's happened to you? You used to not care about anything but video games and movies—important stuff."

"You can't come inside the tape, Adam," Jake warned.

"You'll get in trouble. *I'll* get in trouble."

Adam waved away Jake's concern. He said, "You used to be the coolest one of us." He folded his brawny arms against his chest. "Well, almost. But now you're all messed up. Get rid of all that tiger stuff and let's check out the show. Nothing's gonna happen to the planes while you're gone."

"They're my responsibility," Jake protested.

"You're twelve years old! We're not supposed to have responsibilities yet—we're supposed to have fun."

Peter said, "Adam, even your folks make you do stuff around the house." He had snapped out of his trance and devoured most of the ice cream in his sticky hand.

"Only because they give me an allowance first," Adam shot back.

Jake said, "That's backward. You make a goal, set a date, and follow a plan, then you get your reward." He held up his hands in surrender as Adam raised his fists. "Hey, don't look at me that way. It worked the last time you took a test, didn't it?"

Adam dropped his arms, suddenly lost and defeated. In a hurt voice, he said, "I miss you, dude. I miss doing stuff together, doing nothing together. Just hanging out."

"Well, I got in trouble and then I got inspired and—"

"Yeah, yeah, we already heard your little speech. Save it for him." He pointed to the opposite end of the ring, where Matt the Armpit stood in an air show t-shirt, which he'd already gotten dirty. The kid blinked behind his goggle-like glasses and waved.

Adam thumped Jake in the shoulder and said, "Don't talk to me again until you feel like talking, not reciting all that Tiger Flight stuff."

"What's wrong with believing in something?"

"You're a slacker, just like me," Adam hissed. "You're not supposed to believe in anything but a good time." He stepped over the tape and marched away.

When the confrontation ended, Peter and Vic turned their attention to the planes again. Mesmerized by the sight, they swayed like two trees in the wind. Actually Peter was more like a shrub compared to Vic. Jake knew that with a slight nudge, he'd get these guys as jazzed as he was about the Tiger Flight. He pointed to his chest and then to the aircraft tail fins. "This shield," he said, "is an homage to the Flying Tigers squadron from World War—"

"Come on, guys," Adam shouted from the Lil' Orbits mini-donut stand. "I'm buying."

Peter backed up a few steps, still staring at the planes. Then, as if caught in a tractor beam, he turned and trotted to Adam. Vic's thumbs slowed on the keypad of his microcomputer; Jake knew he had to keep firing out facts to hold Vic's attention.

Adam yelled, "Hey Vic. Back this way, they said we could sit in a real flight simulator. They'll tell us what all the gauges and levers and stuff mean."

Vic glanced down at Jake. "Can I sit in one of the planes?"

"Sorry, man, it's against the pilots' rules. They don't let anyone in these planes unless they invite you personally."

Vic said, "I'll just check out that simulator thing and come back, okay?" He was already backing away.

"Sure," Jake said half-heartedly. "No prob. See you later." He looked past Vic's retreating figure where Adam waited, smiling in triumph. Why were friends such jerks sometimes?

CHAPTER SEVENTEEN

By the time Jake scuffed over to Matt, the Tiger Flight pilots had returned. They were joking with a half dozen other pilots who wore a variety of military uniforms and flight suits. One of these strangers, a square-jawed man in Air Force blues, called Winder a "nasal radiator" instead of a "naval aviator" and Winder kidded back, "At least I'm still flying, Larry—the last time you were wheels-up it was because you'd fallen asleep and your office chair tipped over."

The guys went back and forth like that awhile longer, with Jake and Matt looking on. Clearly the men were good friends even though they'd served in different branches of the military and had flown different kinds of planes. It didn't matter what they flew—what made them like brothers was that they flew at all.

People had begun to wander back from the lunch wagons and line the yellow barricade again. The Tiger Flight broke off their friendly dogfight with the others, stepped over the tape, and spread out to take questions.

Winder stood nearby as Jake told Matt about the Young Eagles program. Normally Jake would've shooed the kid away long ago, but Matt sounded really interested in the twin-tailed tigers and had read up on them, which impressed Jake. Even if the kid was sorta different, his interest in flying made him worth talking to. Besides, the distraction helped push Adam's angry words into the background.

Matt asked Winder, "How did you get that name on your patch?"

"It's a call sign." Winder said. He must've been in a talkative mood from bantering with the other pilots, because he added, "It's a joke, really, at my expense. 'Winder' is short for Sidewinder, the name of a missile." He shook his head at the memory. "I accidentally launched one from my Navy fighter during a training exercise—scared my wingman half to death and earned me the call sign 'Winder' for life."

Jake said, "Gosh, did the missile hit anything?"

"Just open water, somewhere in the Indian Ocean, but it's what I became known for."

Matt pointed at Jake. "Why doesn't he have a call sign?"

Winder reverted to his silent stance, arms folded, weight on his heels. He seemed to be considering something. Finally, he said, "One day, he'll become famous—or infamous—for doing something, and then he'll get his call sign." The pilot tapped the bill of Jake's crew cap. "If he's lucky, it'll be something good."

Jake didn't say anything as Matt wandered away, but he was relieved that his damage to Sunny's plane didn't haunt him for life as his call sign. Still, he flinched at what might have been. "Dent" maybe? Or "Crush"? Geez, that would've been awful.

Remembering the incident in the hangar brought back terrible feelings of guilt, which compounded with the regret he felt for neglecting his friendship with Adam and the others. What do you do when you're suddenly interested in—heck, obsessed with—something your best friend doesn't care about? Get a new best friend? He'd known Adam forever, since daycare.

Before he could puzzle it out, the next visitors piled on the remorse. Debra Mackenzie and her uncle Max greeted the Tiger Flight pilots, and they treated her like a beloved daughter and the burly, gray-haired man like one of their own. Drifting down the reception line, they finally reached Jake.

Max had Fury's overall size with Bones' bulldog build. He had a gray, close-cropped beard and mustache and a penetrating stare, like he could read people's minds. Jake looked down and noticed that Max lacked the last three fingers on his left hand. Only stumps with thick scar tissue emerged from his massive knuckles. Jake tried not to stare.

"So," Max growled, "you're the one who stove in Sunny's wing root."

Shame torched Jake's face and ears. He ducked his head

and said, "I'm sorry about that."

"The guys say you're showing a lot more respect now around my babies."

Jake glanced back at the tiger-striped planes. "You own all these?"

"No, but I treat them like I do."

Debra said, "Uncle Max does all the repair work for the Tiger Flight."

"I know that," Jake snapped. He was glad to have a target for transferring his bad feelings. "You've only told me a hundred times."

Debra took a step back. "What's got into you?"

"Nothing."

Max said, "I didn't mean to get your goat. I just wanted to tell you that everybody's happy with how well you turned out after that rocky start."

Without thinking, Jake asked the first question that popped into his mind: "How can you repair the planes with your hand like that?"

Farther up the line, TC called, "Nice going, Jake. You going to insult his mother next?"

"Sorry," Jake said, his face coloring. "That was way rude of me."

Debra stared at him as if he'd grown a second head, but Max merely shrugged. He said, "I teach aircraft mechanics at

Coosa Valley Technical College, back in Rome. A few years back, a careless student was about to lose his hand to a band saw blade, but I knocked it out of the way at the last second. It cost me three fingers to save five of his. A good trade."

"Wow," Jake said. His stomach lurched as he imagined that kind of sacrifice. To make amends for his testiness, he added, "The great thing about working with Tiger Flight is that I get to meet so many brave guys. Real heroes."

Max shook his massive head. "Just doing my job."

Jake knew he was bordering on rudeness again, but he had to ask, "How, um, *do* you do your job? Not the teaching part; I mean the mechanic part."

Debra blew up at him. Leaning in, jabbing Jake's breastbone, she said, "He does it better than anyone else."

"I was just asking." Jake held up his palms. Then he put his hands behind his back, instantly guilty that he'd displayed all his fingers to a man who'd given up three of his own. Jake felt lower than ever. Since his friends appeared, everything had turned to crap.

Max said calmly, "It's a fair question. Actually some of the precision things that require two good hands are tough for me. I usually hire a student from the college to help out in my workshop, but with school ending for the summer, I'm shorthanded." His smile at the awful pun was dazzling—a flash of chalk-white teeth.

It was the kind of smile that made you smile back without a thought. Jake said, “That joke’s so bad.”

“You gotta keep laughing, kid,” Max said by way of parting. “Don’t let anyone get you down.”

As Max lumbered away, with Debra pulling him to another exhibit—King Kong being led by a pixie—Jake knew it was just what he needed to hear.

The Tiger Flight wasn’t scheduled to fly again until the next morning. To Jake, the pilots looked a little tired from the grueling formation flying and now sweating in the hot afternoon sunshine while chatting to the countless strangers who came by. Dad also looked fatigued from the long day, not to mention sunburned. He’d stopped by a couple of times to supply Jake with icy bottled water and snacks, but Jake always had to step away so he could take care of more visitors. Jake loved, loved, *loved* being the Tiger Flight crew and spokesman. Max’s comments had perked him up; he felt like he could answer questions and pose for pictures for another six hours.

TC tapped his shoulder. “Some of us are hungry again and some of us have to hit the head. You going to be okay if we split for a few minutes?”

“Sure. I can handle this until the end if y’all need to rest.”

“You saying that we’re a bunch of old men?” TC gave him a mock-angry look.

“No, sir! I’m just saying that I’m cool with doing my job

alone till you come back."

TC stretched his back, hands on hips. "Man, I'd give anything to be a kid again. We ain't old, but we ain't twelve anymore either. Okay, crewmember, you've got the duty until we get back." He gave Jake a nod and ushered the other pilots toward the concession stands and port-a-potties.

"Hey, Jake."

Jake turned to see Billy Grant in a snappy outfit of white polo shirt, khakis, and boat shoes. His hair was ruffled stylishly and he had a perfect suntan; he looked like he'd been sailing all day. He crossed one foot over the other and struck a pose against one of the traffic barrels between which the yellow tape was strung.

"Um, hey, Billy." Jake crossed to him. Too bad the Tiger Flight guys had gone. He felt like he needed reinforcements.

Billy said, "I came over to apologize for the way my folks acted awhile back. You know, at the airport. They can be such snobs." He looked around, as if making sure his parents weren't in earshot. "They put a lot of pressure on me to be like them and it makes me crazy and stupid sometimes, so I'm sorry I've been a jerk too. Friends?" He put out his well-groomed hand.

Friends with Billy Grant. Jake remembered the last time he'd entertained that fantasy, right before Billy sneered at him. Still, the dude seemed sincere; he had a pained look in his eyes, as if he was afraid of having his peace offering rejected.

Jake gave in and Billy pumped his arm with grateful enthusiasm. Billy said, "Thanks, you're a good sport. C'mon and tell me about these beautiful planes."

Launching into his spiel, Jake remained tense. He waited for the mockery, the cruel teasing he'd received before, but Billy remained the perfect listener, paying attention and asking smart questions. He urged Jake for more details about the harrowing escape from the hangar, to tell the whole story and not just the boiled-down patter.

Whenever someone else came over to have a look at the planes, Billy said, "Take your time with them. I'll wait—I want to hear what happened next." And he stood patiently, hands clasped in front of him, seemingly oblivious to the stares of pretty girls as they wandered past.

Jake finally finished the story of how he went from a videogame and TV junkie who didn't know anything about planes to the Tiger Flight's spokesman for the weekend, and Billy applauded. Then a worried look crossed his face. He whispered, "I need your help."

"With what?" Jake leaned closer.

Billy said, "I have a secret no one knows about. I'm myopic." Jake frowned at this and Billy clarified, "I'm nearsighted—I can't see details except up close. It's the reason I sit in the front row in class."

Jake asked, "Do you wear glasses or contacts?"

"I hate putting things in my eyes, so I can't wear contacts. And glasses make me look like a dork. What I'm saying is, I can barely see those awesome planes behind you." He squinted past Jake's shoulder. "They're just a blur of orange."

"How can I help?"

"Can I stand beside one of them?" Billy squinted harder.

Jake looked around but didn't spot the Tiger Flight pilots. He said, "I'm not supposed to let anyone inside the tape."

"For safety, right?" Billy nodded emphatically, answering his own question. "I understand. I promise not to touch anything. Please? I'd love to be able to see them the way you do."

Jake looked around again and waved him over the yellow tape. "Come on, hurry."

"Thanks, man," Billy said. "I really appreciate this." He strode up to the nearest one, Sunny's N5695F, and peered at the propeller and nose cone assembly and then up at the closed canopy. He clasped his hands behind his back.

Reassured, Jake turned and saw another group of visitors fast-walking his way. A trio of children aged four to nine broke into a run, pointing and exclaiming, and a half-dozen men and women hurried to catch up. They all beamed at Jake and the planes while they took pictures with their cameras and cell phones.

The questions began in earnest, but nothing Jake hadn't heard before. He answered each one in turn until the four-year-old girl asked, "What's he doing?"

"Who?"

"The boy behind you."

Jake resisted turning around—this group of kids looked like they were ready to hop the tape at any second. He said, "He's looking at the planes up close." Knowing that they would want to do the same, Jake lied, "He's practically blind—it's the only way he can see them."

The nine year old, a stocky boy, said, "Then why's he trying to fly it?"

"Hunh?" Jake whipped around but didn't see Billy. Then he noticed the middle portion of the canopy pushed back and Billy's perfectly tousled head behind the windshield.

The engine coughed once and the propeller began to turn, only ten feet from Jake's face.

CHAPTER EIGHTEEN

Even though the engine couldn't start without the key in Sunny's pocket, and the propeller stopped after one slow revolution, the kids behind Jake were already screeching. Their parents pulled them back and hollered to each other as the reaction rippled across the airport.

Jake ran around the wing and leaped onto the black rectangle. Ready to sit on Billy, punch him, or whatever else he had to do to prevent a worse disaster, he sprang at the cockpit.

Billy was gone.

Either he'd scared himself and ran away or he'd deliberately slipped out in the confusion. Whichever, the damage was done. Jake dropped onto the pilot's seat and turned off the switches Billy had flipped. Despite that no one was in danger, shouts and cries continued to come at him in waves. All his fault.

"What the—" Sunny's face, scary with rage, loomed overhead. "Get out of there!" He looked like he wanted to yank Jake out of the seat, so Jake hopped up before the pilot decided to grab him. Sunny snapped, “Go on, get down.”

Since the pilot remained on the wing walk, Jake had to step onto the copilot seat and deplane from that side. By the time he jumped to the ground, the other Tiger Flight pilots surrounded him. Their looks of anger and deep disappointment were worse than the crowd’s screams. None of them said anything—they just stared Jake down.

Sunny dashed to the tape and reassured people that everything was under control. “Just a little mishap,” he said, “but the planes are safe and secure. It won’t happen again.”

Jake knew that for sure. His bottom lip quivered but he willed himself not to cry. “I’m so sorry,” he blubbered.

“Yeah, chief,” said Fury, fists clenching and unclenching. He was now the embodiment of his call sign. “We’ve heard that tune before.”

TC said, “We trusted you. Why did you do it?”

Any explanation would sound lame, Jake knew, but he tried anyway. “It wasn’t me. This kid—” he cleared his throat “—this kid said he couldn’t see well and promised not to touch anything. I let him in. He was behaving, but then I got distracted by another group and, and—” He covered his face to block out their angry stares. They probably hated him. He’d ruined everything. His breath hiccupped as he fought the urge to bawl. Jake had never felt so pitiful, so unloved.

His head was suddenly cooler—someone had snatched off

his crew cap. He dropped his hands as Sunny, clutching the hat, glared at him.

The pilot's face still showed anger, but his voice had become deadly calm. "I called your father. He's on the way." He waved his arm, motioning Jake toward the yellow tape. "Go on, you're done here."

A condemned prisoner, an exile about to be banished, Jake shuffled past Sunny.

"Step over," the pilot ordered.

Jake complied. He knew a plea of mercy was useless. He'd screwed up so bad, there was no way to make things right. With his last ounce of dignity, he faced them.

Sunny held out his palm and said, "Give me that patch."

Jake gripped the edge of the Tiger Flight patch and tore it from the Velcro tab on the t-shirt. His heart seemed to go with it. Fingers trembling, he handed over the beautiful shield of blue and yellow.

"Nick," Fury said, "he's over here."

Dad appeared by Jake's side. His face showed the same hurt and betrayal as the pilots'.

Squaring his shoulders, Dad said the little speech he'd obviously prepared as he crossed the grounds: "Gentlemen, you're probably sick and tired of apologies from the Skyler family, but I assure you that we're ashamed of Jake's behavior. We'll do whatever's necessary to make things right."

Fury stalked to his plane and jerked out Jake's duffle, which looked puny and misshapen in his grip. He thrust it into Dad's outstretched hand. "Just get him out of here," he muttered.

No one said, "And don't come back," but Jake knew that's what the big man meant.

Designed to succeed. Built by the best. Destined to fly. It had all seemed like the solid truth on the flight from Rome. Jake felt he had turned those beautiful ideas into a pack of lies.

Although he wanted to say goodbye to everyone, he knew what was expected of him: to hang his head and leave them forever. Still, he hadn't heard from one of the pilots, the quiet cowboy who had come to his rescue in the hardware store. The man who had thrown him a lifeline and pulled him into the magical world of the airport. The naval and commercial aviator who'd made it possible for him to regain his self-respect and work his way into everyone's good graces. Jake looked up at him, hoping for one more chance.

Winder only shook his head.

CHAPTER NINETEEN

"Listen," Dad said on the drive home, "you can blame Billy Grant all you want, but you know the responsibility for those planes was yours. You were supposed to be the Pilot in Command."

Jake mumbled, "Yeah, I know." He glanced down at his black t-shirt. The spiny Velcro tab was still there, mocking him with the reminder of everything he'd lost. He tore it off slowly and painfully and also removed the nametag his mom had given him as a gift. Because she was proud of him. Because she believed in him.

The daylight was dying so Dad switched on the truck headlights. He said, "We've got to figure out what to tell your mother."

"That I'm a slacker. An idiot. A loser."

"Hey," Dad shouted, smacking the steering wheel. "That's the end of the pity party. You feel like a loser? Fine—give yourself a good kick in the butt and get over it. Learn your lesson and figure out what you're going to do next."

"I'm not gonna do anything next. I'm done—Sunny said so."

"You're done with them, not with your life." His father took a breath and lowered his voice. "You're twelve years old, buddy. You've got so much living left to do, soon you won't even remember what all the fuss was about—you'll be following a new dream."

"Sure, okay." Jake replayed the movie in his mind of the first time he saw the Tiger Flight, the diamond formation, the salute. Would any other dream grab him like that?

Dad asked with exaggerated patience, "So what do you think we should tell her?"

"The truth."

"Good boy. And?"

Jake grimaced. "And wipe out my emotional bank account with her too. You'll have to scoot over and make some room for me in her doghouse."

His comment seemed to jar his father; maybe it reminded him of what kind of trouble he could be in too, by going to bat for Jake. Dad fell into a long, brooding silence.

Mom stepped into the garage as soon as the overhead door rolled up. Jake tried to read the expression on her face as she squinted into the headlights, but he could only guess: somewhere between shock and relief. He buzzed down his window and waved to her so she wouldn't fear the worst.

As soon as Jake and his dad stepped down from the truck, she asked, "What happened?"

"I messed up and got fired," Jake said, using the words he'd rehearsed on the drive back. "I let this kid from school touch one of the planes and—"

"Jake," his father warned.

"I was getting to it." He picked up his story again: "And he tried to start the engine and caused a big panic." His mom's hands went to her mouth and he hurried to finish. "No one got hurt, but the pilots were still really upset and made me leave."

Mom hurried over and hugged him. She whispered, "I know that was scary for you."

When she released him, he said hopefully, "So you're not mad?"

"Are you crazy?" Hands on hips, she reverted back to the imperial queen. "Of course I'm angry at you. You betrayed our trust and the trust those pilots had in you."

"Then why'd you just hug me?"

"Because I can tell you're upset."

Dad quipped, "Maybe he wanted to be punished first and hugged after."

Mom turned on him. "Nick, you're not helping. It was your bright idea to let him go in the first place. Why don't you get your gear and we'll talk later."

Dad grabbed the two duffle bags from the truck and stalked

inside as Jake looked on in stunned silence. He'd counted on having his father there to back him up if things got rough.

Jake followed his mother into the kitchen saying, "Don't blame Dad. He told the guys how ashamed he was and apologized for the whole family."

"You don't have to fight his battles. Your father isn't the issue here—the issue is you."

"I told everyone I'm sorry a thousand times. I wish I could change things, but I can't."

Mom sat ramrod straight at the head of the kitchen table. "Saying you're sorry isn't enough. All the punishments from before are back in place: no TV, no Internet, no video games."

Jake had been expecting that. In a way, he felt relieved. There were only so many things they could take from him. Having been through it once before, he knew he'd survive. Besides, summer vacation was coming, which meant spending his days with Adam, whose mother didn't work and who would spoil both of them with daily treats. At Adam's house, there were no rules except to have fun. Jake only hoped his friend wouldn't make him beg for forgiveness before they got down to the serious business of figuring out which movies to watch and in what order.

But Mom wasn't finished. "One other thing," she said. "Starting next week, when you're on summer break, I'll telecommute."

"What's that?"

"It means I'll be working from home—where I can keep my eye on you."

"But what about me going over to Adam's?"

"Nope." She shook her head forcefully. "You're grounded all summer."

On the last Monday of the school year, Jake trudged into math class and slumped in his seat. He didn't notice who else was there. Ever since Mom had made her pronouncement, he'd suffered from tunnel vision, unable—unwilling, really—to see anything around him. He felt hollow inside, a Plexiglas shell over an empty cockpit. Staring dead ahead, he saw Billy Grant six rows up. Billy remained focused on whatever Mrs. K was saying to him from her desk. He didn't glance back at Jake, not even to smirk.

A soft voice beside Jake said, "I heard what happened." Debra patted his shoulder, but he didn't feel her sympathy, only the dull vibrations from her fingertips.

To his left, a math book thudded onto the desk and Adam fell into his chair. He said, "What's up?"

Debra asked, "Jake? Are you in there? Do you want to tell him or do you want me to?"

"I don't care," Jake said. His voice sounded far off, like when he wore the radio headset but didn't hold the microphone close enough to his mouth. Everything, it seemed, reminded him of Tiger Flight, of what he'd thrown away.

Adam asked, "So, what happened?"

Debra said, "Somebody sneaked into the cockpit on Saturday and tried to start the engine. People got scared and ran away but nobody was hurt. On Sunday, Tiger Flight still drew the biggest crowds—Uncle Max replaced Jake as the crew for the day."

"Replaced? Did they fire you?"

Jake realized Adam had addressed the question to him. He droned, "They did." His right hand involuntarily touched the spot on his chest where he'd surrendered the Tiger Flight patch.

"So you're through with planes and stuff?" Adam nudged him and Jake rocked like a bobble-head doll.

"I am." He didn't know if it was true or not, but he was sure the Tiger Flight was through with him.

Adam said, "Then I guess you're one of us again." He sounded relieved, happy even. "I've got dibs on picking the first thirty movies we watch at my place. Then you can choose the next five."

Welcome back to Slacker World. Jake couldn't get too excited about that. His tunnel vision continued to focus on the back of Billy's head. Jake knew he could tell Adam and his other friends that Billy had been the cause of his troubles and maybe they'd beat the snot out of Mr. Perfect. But ratting out

Billy wouldn't solve any problems; he'd only create an enemy for life. Maybe by *not* naming names he'd make Billy owe him big time.

The thought caused Jake to smile for the first time since Saturday afternoon. With his smile, the tunnel vision lessened; he could see a larger piece of the classroom. Smiling back at him was Matt, a fellow lover of planes. Jake felt bad that he'd thought mean things about him—the boy was all right. Matt held a glossy piece of paper filled out with careful block letters, the Young Eagles form.

Well, good for him, Jake thought. Maybe he'll grab the dream and do better than I did. He gave the kid a thumbs up.

Finally, Jake turned to face Adam. He said, "I've got bad news about summer vacation."

CHAPTER TWENTY

Despite everything that had happened, each night before he went to sleep and every morning when he woke up Jake still thought about flying. It was Friday evening and the school year was over—seventh grade would start in August when he would be thirteen, finally a teenager. He knew he should've been excited about that, but he wasn't. Instead, he recalled the giddy flip-flopping of his stomach during wingovers and G-turns, the illusion of going faster and faster the closer the plane flew to the ground, the vibrations that tingled his hands and feet while taxiing the tiger up to the runway and back.

In the past, those memories had lulled him to sleep. Not tonight.

His head was too busy, full of thoughts about how to get back what he'd lost. He knew he wouldn't have much else to do besides think now that summer vacation had begun. With Mom "telecommuting" and all forms of entertainment off limits except reading, he was sure to get a lot of thinking done.

Maybe that was Mom's plan all along. She expected him to dwell on his mistakes and make a commitment to do things differently from now on.

As he lay awake, staring at the aircraft pictures he'd taped all over his walls, it only took a second of thinking to reach that point. Jake 1.0 would've drifted off into daydreams, but as Jake 2.0 he'd taught himself to focus. And it was obvious what he had to do. Time for another new version of himself: Jake 3.0.

With his last upgrade from Jake 1.0 to 2.0, he'd eliminated pointless fantasies, most truth-bending, and outright lying, but obviously that wasn't enough. Jake 3.0 would stop being so desperate to please the Billy Grants of the world, the cool crowd. What did his mom call that willingness to do anything—even to play the fool—in order to be liked? "Ingratiating," that was it. "Bootlicking" was Dad's take on such behavior.

Okay, no more ingratiating and no licking boots. Great. It would keep him out of the kind of troubles he'd had at the air show, but it didn't solve his current problem. On his dresser, he kept the page of notebook paper where he'd written down his goal, his plan of action, and the date he intended to achieve the goal. He still wanted to fly more than anything, and the best teachers were only a mile up the highway. Too bad they wouldn't bother with him anymore.

How would Jake 3.0 handle this? It would be the opposite of the groveling, whining, toady route Jake 2.0 would take.

Jake 3.0 would show himself as worthy of another chance. He would work so hard and with such dedication the pilots would admit he deserved forgiveness. Even if they didn't give in, he would follow through, finish what he started, and be better for it. So…how to show them he was worthy when they wouldn't even let him near the hangar?

After some more thought, he had a plan. He wrote it down on a fresh sheet of paper along with his new goal and a date two months away. Putting it into action would require the best speech of his life, but he now believed in Jake 3.0 with all his heart. In no time, he fell asleep.

On Saturday over a lunch of tuna fish sandwiches and milk, Mom said, "Absolutely not."

Jake hadn't asked the others whose permission he would need. If Mom vetoed the idea, it was DOA, as the TV doctors say: dead on arrival.

He knew she would be the biggest challenge. The problem at the air show had confirmed something in her mind—what was it that made her so set against his dream every step of the way? Dad had said, "When it's the right time, she'll tell you." Maybe he needed to speed up the clock. Get it out into the open and find a way for it to help his cause.

Jake took another bite of tuna sandwich, even though his mind was racing so fast that he didn't taste the food. She carried a secret from her past, something not even Dad would tell him about. Obviously something about flying, about planes.

She narrowed her eyes and said, "What are you up to?"

"What do you mean?"

"I mean, you gave up too easily. You spin this big, elaborate plan to get back those pilots' respect and I say 'no' and you drop it? That's not like you."

He frowned at her. "You're saying you want me to try again?"

"I'm just wondering where's your spirit. The Jake I know would come right back with pleading and groveling, appealing to my emotions. You'd point out how much better you did in school since the pilots taught you to set goals and stick to them."

Curious to see where this led, he asked, "Then what would you say?"

Mom seemed to be getting into this, laying out a strategy to change her own mind. It was weird, but he wanted her to keep going. She leaned forward confidentially and told him, "I'd say, 'I'm proud of you for that, but you still haven't learned your lesson about taking responsibility."

"You mean being a Pilot in Command of my life?"

She thought about that a minute, maybe trying to see it from all sides to make sure she wasn't walking into a trap. "Well… yes, you could put it that way."

Jake said, "And then I'd thank you for the nametag you

made for me, say how proud I was to wear it, and try to get you to see how everything fit together."

She nodded, going with the flow. "Yeah, that's right, and I'd hug you and say, 'I'm sorry, but my decision is final.'"

"And that would be that," Jake concluded.

"Yes." She seemed pleased that they'd worked together on this, even though they ended up where they'd started.

It was like when Dad was teaching him chess or card games. He'd lay out the most likely moves, how the opponent would probably react, and how those decisions would lead to victory or defeat. Jake said, "Okay, Mom, what you're telling me is to give up. I'm in checkmate—there's no way to win."

She now looked disappointed. "There's always a chance to win. You should never give up."

Jake took a swallow of milk and wiped his mouth. He said, "So, now you're going to explain how to get my way?"

"Absolutely not," his mom said for the second time.

He laughed—they'd gone full circle yet again. Still, she'd left the door open for him to keep trying. She seemed to be demanding that he do so. The secret was to discover her secret.

On Monday morning, the first day of summer vacation, Jake got to see firsthand what his mother did for a living: write countless e-mails and talk on the phone to people he could tell she didn't like. Her job was beyond boring and she grumbled to herself a lot. It reinforced his decision to become a pilot, to spend his days doing something he loved.

He continued to wonder about her past, something that had happened before she knew Dad, something to do with flying. She never talked about growing up, and her parents—his Grandma and Grandpa Berkowitz—didn't tell stories about "back in the day." Amazingly, they were still focused on what they were going to do tomorrow and the next day. He would've asked them about Mom, but they were on a hiking tour of Italy for another month.

So, research was needed. She'd packed up his computer and changed the password for the one they kept in the family room. However, her laptop from work sat open on the cluttered desk in the study, since she had all of those e-mails to read and send. He crept past the study doorway a couple of times each hour and there she was, hunched over the laptop, typing and barking commands into the phone at the same time. The imperial queen ruled her ten galaxies with a no-nonsense voice and a high-speed Internet connection.

Fortunately, she drank a lot of coffee and loved to gaze out the kitchen window while she sipped it. Jake listened from his room as she clicked off the portable phone and then headed to the other end of the house for a refill. He dashed into the study, figuring he had fifteen minutes before she returned.

She had a web-search program open on the laptop, so he

entered a bunch of keywords, including "Berkowitz," "plane," "aircraft," and "flying." Over 15,900 hits came up. Jake groaned. Who knew that Berkowitz was such a common name?

He scanned each page of listings and clicked on a few news stories, but they were all recent accounts. Around page 10, he heard the kitchen faucet turn on as she rinsed her cup. He closed the program and then reopened it so she'd have to look in the search history to discover his efforts. Not that she would ever suspect that anything was going on.

Thereafter, he settled into a routine, enjoying a book in his room while keeping his ears open. A fresh pot of coffee always brewed in the kitchen, and every few hours, Mom would make a beeline for it. Then, he'd enter his keywords and scan another ten pages or so of hits.

On Friday, he found her secret.

It happened accidentally. He'd gone to a page about an air show because some famous flying Berkowitz appeared there, but again the time period wasn't right. On a sidebar were links to other air show sites and, out of curiosity, he tried one. That led him to another, which threaded to a third. He knew he was wasting time, but he couldn't resist the subject of planes and pilots. The next site he pulled up discussed heroism in flight, pilots who had rescued people or landed their planes safely against huge odds, sometimes making the ultimate sacrifice to protect others.

One story from back in the 1980s detailed a military pilot at an air show whose engine caught fire in mid-flight. Although his wingman advised him to eject, the pilot radioed back that he wouldn't let his jet crash into the crowd of onlookers. He steered the crippled aircraft away from the spectators and into a deserted field. There, the engine exploded and the resulting fireball killed him, but he saved an estimated 200 lives. The pilot's name was Major Robert Burnside. Jake remembered hearing that last name before. His mom's father and mother sometimes called themselves B&B because Grandpa's last name was Berkowitz and Grandma's maiden name was Burnside.

He checked the clock on the laptop and thought he had a few minutes to spare. After typing in Robert Burnside and Grandma's name—Emily—and clicking the search button, he discovered a newspaper story about the pilot's bravery and his funeral a week later. Listed among the attendees was Major Burnside's sister Emily along with her husband and their twelve-year-old daughter, Susan Berkowitz.

Jake's mom.

He heard his mother's footsteps coming from the kitchen. Maybe he could've escaped from the study, but he decided to wait. It was show time.

She ambled into the room, and he swiveled the office chair around to face her. "Hey," she said, sounding more surprised than mad, "what are you doing?"

"Mom, were you really close to your uncle, Major Robert?"

She took a step back and held onto the doorframe. After a long moment, she murmured, "Rob. I always called him Uncle Rob. How did you know?"

"I surfed the Net. Sorry, I know I'm not supposed to touch a computer all summer, but I wanted to find out what happened when you were a kid."

His mother tried to see around his shoulder to the laptop screen. "What was on the Internet about me?"

"Just a mention of you at his funeral."

She leaned against the open door, shoulders slumped, head down. "That was a long time ago," she said.

"Did you see it happen?"

Her jaw clenched and she squeezed her always-sad eyes shut and nodded. Twin tears etched her cheeks.

Softly, he asked, "And that's why you've been against me all along?"

"I haven't been against you, honey," she said as she wiped her face with her fingertips. "Just the thought of you flying."

"But he was a hero. He saved 200 people—maybe you and your parents included." Jake paused and followed the logic of that. "That means he saved me too, and every other kid who came from that crowd. And if we have kids, it means he saved them, and on and on. Thousands of people, and he's saving more all the time."

She rolled over another chair and sat beside him. Taking his hands in her damp, icy grip, she said, "But I don't want you to be a hero, I want you to be alive. Just like I want Uncle Rob to still be alive."

"The article said he was also a decorated Marine fighter pilot in Vietnam." Jake pointed to the article, which featured a photo of Major Burnside in his Marine aviator uniform.

"He was my hero," she said, patting his hands, "before he became everybody else's. Uncle Rob was a great man, brave and kind. He never swaggered—he just had this aura about him that he could do anything." She started to cry again. "You look like him, same eyes, same sweet smile."

"You think?" Jake studied the photograph. If he grew up to be half that handsome, he'd be thrilled.

Mom sniffled and said, "I remember asking him one time, a few months before the air show, why he liked to fly planes so much. He said that from the time he was ten or so it was all he ever wanted to do. He saw a movie about pilots—*Twelve O'clock High*—and he just knew."

"He grabbed his dream," Jake said. "Like I did."

His mother pulled a few tissues from a box nearby and dried her red-rimmed eyes. Clearing her throat, she said, "You know, I thought that if you kept going on and on about flying, I would tell you the story of his crash to scare you—scare you so bad you'd give up your dream. But you understood the real lessons from Uncle Rob's life. His heroism, his sacrifice. Who wouldn't be proud of such a man?" When she smiled at him, her eyes looked brighter. They had lost a little of their sorrowful shadows. She said, "I'm glad you found his story first."

Jake reached over and hugged her. She looked like she needed it; he did too. With his head against her shoulder, he asked, "What happens now, Mom?"

"We call your father and then we call Max Mackenzie," she said. "Pitch them your plan and see if they'll go for it."

CHAPTER TWENTY-ONE

Starting the following week, Jake biked over to Max Mackenzie's place after lunch to assist the aircraft mechanic with tasks that required two hands. As often as possible, Jake wanted to help on the jobs Max did for the Tiger Flight. Max agreed to keep Jake's role a secret, but, in return, he wanted to be the one to surprise the pilots with the news when the time was right.

Jake was thrilled to learn about the care and maintenance of aircraft. Although he missed hanging out with Adam, this was much more exciting than watching movie marathons every day.

The first real test of keeping the secret safe came a few weeks after he started work. Sunny was flying in that Saturday afternoon to replace some parts in N5695F that Max had promised would be ready. Unfortunately, Jake was slower and less sure of himself than the mechanic's usual student-help, so he would be grinding flanges right up until the minute Sunny landed. Then he'd have to hide and wait for the pilot to leave.

As Jake biked as fast as he could to Max's farm, traveling over two-lane back roads, he rehearsed in his mind the steps he needed to follow to remove the burrs from the metal and measure the dimensions for accuracy. About a quarter mile from the farm, the usual patrol car sat on the shoulder just below a rise in the road, a hump that joyriding teenagers liked to speed over. Supposedly, if you went fast enough your wheels would leave the ground for a second. Everybody, it seemed, wanted to fly.

On most days, Jake stopped and chatted with Deputy Howard, who manned the radar. Today he was in a hurry, though, so he merely waved as he shot past.

A burst from the police siren brought him to a sideways, sliding halt. He looked through the windshield and saw Deputy Howard motion for him to come over.

With a quick glance at his watch and a fearful thought about the work he still had to do, Jake dismounted and walked his bike back to the patrol car.

The deputy, a stocky, balding man in his early forties, asked Jake, "Where's the fire? You don't have time to shoot the breeze with your old pal?"

"I'm late getting to Mr. Mackenzie's place."

Deputy Howard glanced at his dashboard clock. "Looks like you're early." He grinned at Jake. "You haven't been exceeding the speed limit, have you?"

"Maybe a little—for a bike anyway."

"Well you watch yourself. We got all kinds of maniacs driving around lately. Kids hot-rodding, people talking on their cell phones, not watching where they're going." He shook his head. "Other stuff too. There was a bank robbery downtown today—you hear about that? And Tennessee sent word that two prisoners escaped. Plus the full moon tonight is gonna bring out all the crazies." He took a sip of coffee, but before Jake could excuse himself, he went on, "I busted a punk yesterday for shoplifting a bike; he tried to roll it out of the store like nobody would notice."

Jake nodded and stole another look at his watch. It took two more minutes for the lawman to run out of steam. Jake wished him a good day and pumped his pedals, hoping to get over the rise before the deputy decided to tell him about every arrest he'd ever made.

The road bordered Max Mackenzie's property, which was dominated by a grass landing strip as pretty as a putting green, with his ranch house on one side and a workshop where Jake was helping the mechanic on the other. He hid his bike behind the long, aluminum-sided shop so Sunny wouldn't see it, and he went inside. Normally he would've dropped by the house to check on Max, but time was zipping past like one of Deputy Howard's speeders.

Jake shut the workshop door behind him and smelled cutting oil and metal as he put on his goggles, earplugs, gloves, and heavy smock. He inspected the next flange that needed smoothing, his thumb rubbing over the jagged burrs. After switching on the electric grinder, he applied some rosin and worked the steel rim against the fast-spinning wheel. Sparks shot out wherever the metal touched the coarse stone, the bitter odor of heated steel jabbed his nostrils, and a horrendous grating noise penetrated the foam plugs.

The expression "Keep your nose to the grindstone" now made a lot more sense. It was hard, hot, smelly work—anyone who kept at it was worthy of respect. That was his plan anyway.

After he ground each steel rim smooth and measured it to make sure it was sized correctly, he lifted off his goggles, cleared the fogged lenses, and wiped sweat from his eyes. He also removed the earplugs so he could listen for an airplane engine, fearing that Sunny would show up early. Nothing so far.

Max hadn't come over to work alongside him, which was out of the ordinary. Jake looked forward to the mechanic's lessons and counted on his feedback. He hoped he was doing everything right.

His watch showed two minutes to 4:00. As he was stacking the finished pieces in a box, he heard Sunny's engine. Even though his ears still rang from the constant grinding, he knew the sound of a twin-tailed tiger like he knew his own voice.

Jake couldn't help himself, he had to see the landing. He cracked the door wide enough to witness the tiger-striped plane touch down on the grass airstrip. The two back wheels—the "main mounts," he reminded himself—eased onto the earth together, and then the nose descended slowly until that wheel kissed the ground, a perfect landing. The plane taxied past the house and workshop to the far end of the runway and then turned around so Sunny could take off in the direction he'd come.

Retreating behind a curtain of oilcloth, Jake hid from the machining area in an alcove set aside for working with paints and solvents. He waited, holding his breath, in case Sunny checked the workshop before trying the main house.

Sure enough, the shop door opened wide and Sunny called, "Max?" Jake then heard a metallic rattle and he knew the pilot was inspecting the box of parts he'd finished. Booted footsteps grew distant again—Sunny had gone back outside.

Jake eased the curtain aside and made sure he was alone before stepping out. He tiptoed to the now-open door and peeked around the frame.

Sunny, clad in his flight suit, was striding toward the main house. "Max?" he called again.

Max's shiny white pickup truck caught Jake's eye. The truck was parked near the front door, which was odd since Max always kept it around the side. It had been moved since Jake had gone to work on the parts.

From behind the truck, a bearded man appeared. He was dressed in an orange jumpsuit, like a prison inmate on TV crime shows. The man pointed a twin-barreled shotgun at Sunny, who halted at the edge of the airfield closest to the house. "Down on the ground," the stranger ordered.

Sunny put his hands up. He said, "Where's Max?"

"Shut up. I said to get on the ground." He gestured downward with the long barrels of the gun and Sunny knelt in the short grass, hands still held high.

Jake wondered if the shotgun was Max's. If this was one of the escapees that Deputy Howard mentioned, the other one might be somewhere close by. What had they done to Max?

He smelled cigarette smoke in the workshop. Glancing back he saw the rear door had been opened. Adrenaline fired his heart into overdrive. He ran toward his hiding place in the alcove.

From the shadows, two huge, strong hands clamped around his upper arms like pliers. Jake wanted to shout, but he was so startled that no sound came out. He felt hot breath beside his ear as a man whispered, "Gotcha."

The convict lifted Jake with ease and hollered, "Hey, Vance, I got the kid the old man told us about."

Vance shouted back from across the airstrip, "Bring him out, Tony. I've got Han Solo covered."

Tony didn't even grunt as he carried Jake in his outstretched arms across the workshop, heading to the front door. Jake kicked his feet uselessly in midair—he'd never felt so small and helpless in his life.

CHAPTER TWENTY-TWO

Jake knew that somehow he had to break free. If he could lead them away from Sunny, he thought, maybe the pilot could get back to his plane and radio for help.

On the way to the workshop entrance, Tony hauled Jake between the pair of electric grinders. Elevated as Jake was, his hands were at the level of the green start and red stop buttons. He flicked his right hand sideways and slapped the green button. The grindstone hummed to life, distracting Tony, who lowered his arms. Jake heaved his weight to the right and Tony stumbled with him. The huge convict banged against the grinder.

Jake shoved his elbow, which Tony still clutched, directly at the grindstone. As he hoped, Tony's wrist was in the way. The spinning stone caught the orange sleeve and sucked it into the gear works.

Tony released Jake, shrieking as he tried to free his arm. Acrid smoke from singed cloth and skin poured from the grinder. His hand seemed to disappear into the machine as he screamed, but Jake saw that he'd drawn it into his sleeve. As the cloth continued to vanish, his balled fist kept sliding farther inside the arm of the jumpsuit, like the lump of a rat going down a snake's throat.

Outside, Vance shouted, "What's going on?"

Tony slapped blindly for the off switch. Jake kicked the green button on the other grinder, grabbed Tony's other arm as it flailed, and with all his might shoved it against the second grindstone. The orange cuff caught under the wheel. Instantly, the rapid chewing began on Tony's left sleeve as well. He kicked in panic just like Jake had a moment ago. The inmate cried out, looking from one struggling arm to the other and then at Jake, eyes wide with fear.

Jake figured the material would burn away or rip free before the grinders ate Tony's hands. Vance shouted that he was coming to help, so Jake dashed out the back door to his bike. He pedaled around the side of the workshop closest to the aircraft, hoping he'd see Sunny running that way. Instead, the pilot lay still, face first on the ground near the house.

There had been no shot, so Vance must've knocked Sunny out with the gun. Inside the workshop, one grinder and then the other quit and Tony's cries for help became curses as he told Vance what he was going to do to Jake when he caught him.

Jake was on his own now. No way could he pedal to safety—

one blast of the shotgun would finish him. He needed a shield.

Biking as fast as he could to the plane, he felt as if a huge bull's-eye was painted on his back. He kept waiting for Vance to shoot, but from the arguing in the workshop, he could tell the convict was occupied with freeing Tony. Apparently the grinders had eaten so much fabric that Tony was forced to strip out of what was left of his jumpsuit.

Jake dropped the cycle behind the plane, jumped onto the wing walk, and then climbed inside the cockpit. He slid the seat up so he could reach everything and snatched Sunny's keys off the top of the instrument panel. When he punched the starter, the engine roared to life immediately; the propeller spun itself into a blur in front of the windshield. Air rocketed back into his face.

He increased the throttle and taxied as fast as he could down the right side of the airstrip, where Sunny had lined it up. He hated leaving his friend behind, but he'd just get himself captured again—or get them both killed—if he tried to pull Sunny inside the plane.

Jake wished he knew how to take off, but he hadn't progressed that far in his lessons. All he could do was taxi to safety. The situation was so insane it almost made him laugh.

Vance ran through the doorway of the workshop, aiming the shotgun at the plane. Then he stopped. His expression changed from murderous to puzzled. He stared at Sunny's unconscious form on the ground and then back at the plane as if he couldn't figure out how it could be moving.

Jake steered farther to the right, so close to the workshop that Vance dove back inside to avoid the wing. The con rolled over and came up firing. Buckshot punched through the fuselage and canopy on the copilot side and a few pellets ruptured the windshield. The plane began to shudder—the propeller must've been damaged as well. Jake grasped the yoke tight, just to have something to hang on to, and the vibrations made his whole body shake. His teeth rattled, but that was also from fear.

He increased his speed a moment before the second shotgun blast destroyed what was left of the co-pilot side of the cockpit, shattering instrumentation and drilling through to the engine. Oily smoke now mixed with the air blowing back at Jake.

A third shot would either hit him or finish off Sunny's plane. He braced for it, but then remembered the old-fashioned shotgun had two barrels. Hopefully Vance didn't have any spare shells. Jake slid shut what was left of the canopy to deflect the smoke from his eyes. He glanced back and saw two men running after him, one in orange waving a shotgun, the other stripped down to his gray underwear. They dropped farther and farther behind. Escaping at 15 mph was just fast enough. When Jake reached the main road and kept going, leaving a thick fog of black smoke in his wake, they quit the chase and headed back to Max's.

Luckily, he had the road to himself. He could just imagine

one of the teen hotrods thundering up behind him. Jake hoped Deputy Howard had heard the shots on the other side of the rise and was coming to investigate. Approaching the hump—now at 10 mph as the engine began to sputter—would take forever, and Sunny and Max were still in terrible danger.

He put on his headset and switched to the discreet frequency favored by the Tiger Flight. The hump slowly drew nearer. He felt as if the plane was standing still and the world was scrolling toward him at a snail's pace. "Mayday, mayday," he shouted into the microphone. "November 5695 Foxtrot in trouble."

TC's voice came through, calm and cool. "Identify yourself," he commanded.

"This is Jake Skyler."

"What are you doing on this frequency?"

"I'm taxiing Sunny's plane away from Max Mackenzie's place. Two convicts are there with a shotgun. They knocked Sunny out. I don't know what they did to Max."

After Jake quickly explained why he was at Max's, TC's voice crackled in his headset. "We'll contact Fixed Based Operations and have them call 911."

"I'm heading to the police right now," Jake said. He was fighting against the vibrations and losing—the aircraft was shaking itself apart. First he busted Sunny's wing root and now the entire aircraft. No matter how long he worked, he'd never be able to pay for a new plane.

TC said, “I’ve got the flight off my wing. We’re inbound, your location. Stay put, Jake. Stay safe. Tiger 1 out.”

At last, Jake crested the rise. Deputy Howard climbed from his car with a stunned look on his face as Jake manhandled the smoking, shuddering, shot-up wreck of N5695F to a halt in the field alongside the road and killed what was left of the engine.

The lawman called, “When I clocked you at eight miles an hour, I knew you weren’t an ordinary car.”

Jake shoved the canopy backward and shouted, “Call for backup!”

It took another precious minute to explain the situation. Deputy Howard hurried to his car and summoned the dispatcher on his radio. He leaned out and said, “They just got a 911 call about this too. Units are on the way.”

Over the aircraft radio, Jake heard TC giving instructions to the Tiger Flight. Help was coming from the air as well. Jake only hoped his efforts hadn’t been too little, too late. Another saying he now understood all too well.

Deputy Howard yelled, “Sit tight. I’m going to get a closer—” He stared at the radar reading on his dashboard and braced his hands against the steering wheel.

A bright white pickup truck flew over the rise, wheels spinning as it became airborne for a moment before bouncing back to earth. It sped by so fast that the patrol car shook. Looking into the back window of the truck, Jake saw two men, one in an orange jumpsuit at the wheel and the other in a gray t-shirt. No sign of Sunny and Max—at least they hadn't been taken hostages. On the other hand, maybe the convicts did something to them before leaving. Jake slammed his fists against the smoking instrument panel as he watched the white truck zoom up the road.

Deputy Howard's tires spit gravel as he whirled around in pursuit. Blue lights flashed and his siren howled. The sound died away fast as he shot up the road, but he was so far behind the inmates he might never catch up.

The road was a straight gray strip that bordered open fields for miles. Jake had an excellent view of the truck increasing its lead over the deputy. No other police cars were in sight. He contacted the Tiger Flight again. "This is November 5695 Foxtrot. The convicts are getting away, heading east in a white Ford pickup. There are two of them in the cab."

TC said, "I have a visual. Tiger Flight, make left break, head-on run on the truck. Follow my lead."

Jake blurted, "How can you see them? I can't see you."

"Look up." The voice came from Bones, who was with Fury in Tiger 4.

Three tiger-striped planes blasted out of the sunshine in a trail formation, one after the other. They descended rapidly, sweeping down toward the road and the oncoming pickup until they were only ten feet off the ground.

This was an awesome game of chicken: three planes versus a truck. The convicts blinked first. A stream of smoke shot from beneath the truck tires as Vance braked hard and the Ford skidded sideways. It spun 360 degrees and tumbled into a drainage ditch along the shoulder. The Tiger Flight ascended, soaring over the crippled pickup and the approaching patrol car.

Deputy Howard stopped near the wreck and jumped out, gun drawn, but neither of the convicts put up a fight. They could barely climb out of the cab. At that moment, prison probably seemed like a much friendlier place than the outside world.

TC led the flight past Jake. They rocked their wings as they flew by.

Fury said over Jake's headset, "Nice work, chief."

CHAPTER TWENTY-THREE

Jake stood alone outside the closed doors of the Tiger Flight hangar. He looked at the banner with the blue and yellow shield, the twin-tailed, winged tiger, and the lightning bolt. This time though, instead of sneaking in, he waited for his cue.

From inside, a military band struck up a fanfare of brass and drums, and the doors slowly parted as if by magic. The magicians were Gabriel and Drew, each one pulling his door aside in perfect synchronicity with the other. They looked sharp in their Tiger Flight crew uniforms of black and olive drab. Jake wore a tan flight suit and boots, gifts from the two teens. On his head perched a gift from Sunny: the black Tiger Flight cap the pilot had worn on the day Jake taxied for help.

Sunny had suffered a concussion from the whack Vance gave him with the shotgun. Max had fared better, having only been tied up for a few hours. When the convicts were interrogated after their capture, they blamed Jake for everything. Indeed, they were eager to return to prison where they only had to worry about other inmates, not kids armed with electric grinders or dive-bombing planes painted like tigers.

The opening created by the crewmembers revealed a red carpet down the center of the hangar. On either side stood everyone Jake knew: Mom in her sharpest business suit and Dad in a jacket and tie, his friends from class—Debra, Matt, Adam, Peter, and Vic—well scrubbed (even Matt) and in their Sunday best, Mrs. Kirby, his other teachers, and the principal from his school, the staff from Fixed Based Operations, Deputy Howard, and Jake's neighbors. Reporters and cameramen from the newspapers and local TV stations filmed him, shot flash pictures, and recorded the scene in notebooks. The mayor, the city council, and other local political celebrities were on hand, including Billy's parents. Even Billy, standing beside them, looked impressed. He also looked smaller than before.

After the two crewmembers pulled the doors entirely open, they snapped to attention on either side and the band, positioned beneath the windows through which Jake had escaped a lifetime ago, began a stirring, patriotic march. Jake adjusted the brim of his cap, took a deep breath, and slowly entered the hangar with measured steps.

A small stage had been erected at the end of the red carpet. There, in their flight suits and caps, stood the pilots of the Tiger Flight—Bones, Fury, Sunny, TC, and Winder—along with Max. Sunny wore his ball cap a little larger than usual to accommodate the puffy scar on his right temple. Behind these men, arranged in a semicircle the way Jake had found them when his adventure began, were the four tigers, the orange and white polished to a high shine, their black stripes seeming to ripple with power. Max and Jake and the others had worked almost nonstop to repair Sunny's plane. The cash reward Jake and the Tiger Flight had received for helping to capture the inmates paid the repair bills that the insurance company didn't cover, with some left over.

Jake exchanged smiles with his parents and the others as he marched up the aisle and onto the stage. He went down the row, shaking hands with each pilot in turn. Even stoic Winder grinned while pumping Jake's arm. Jake returned to the center of the stage and stood at attention facing the pilots.

When the music ended, Sunny stepped out of the line of pilots, holding a slim, black portfolio. He spoke into the wireless microphone clipped onto his flight suit, and his voice boomed from speakers mounted around the hangar. "We have gathered here today to thank a young man who never gave up. Jake Skyler grabbed his dream and didn't let go, even when it would've been reasonable to do so. He faced opposition at every turn. He made mistakes along the way. But he kept learning about himself and what he was made of. He came to believe with all his heart what so many of us sometimes forget—that we are designed to succeed. We can do anything if we'll only set our goals and follow our plans."

He raised his fingers to the swollen scar left by Vance's blow and looked Jake in the eye. His voice softened as he said, "On the way toward following his plan, he was tested by a terrible situation that had nothing to do with chasing his dream, but everything to do with demonstrating his character: brave and resourceful. No one sets out to become a hero. Some of us, though, have a once-in-a-lifetime chance to show just how much we will do for others, even at extreme risk to ourselves."

Sunny opened the portfolio and held it in front of him. He glanced at its contents and his voice boomed again. "Many of you attended the ceremony at City Hall yesterday, when the mayor gave Jake the key to the city and a trust fund for college. Now, it's our turn. To honor Jake's extraordinary heroism, the pilots of the Tiger Flight are using our reward money and calling in a lot of favors to send Jake and his parents on an all-expense-paid trip to the Air and Space Museum in Washington, DC, with a special private tour there, so they can learn about the other brave men and women who have conquered the skies and journeyed beyond our world."

The audience whistled and clapped, and Sunny handed over a parchment-like certificate from the portfolio. Jake's hands trembled as he scanned the details about the trip to Washington. The roundtrip flight, where Jake was invited to sit in the cockpit. The hotel and restaurant reservations. The private tour of the museum led by a two-time commander of the Space Shuttle. Even a limo service that would take Jake and his parents wherever they wanted to go. He turned and looked at Mom and Dad in the front row. They clapped even harder.

Sunny raised a hand, quieting the crowd. "But if that were all, we would've made our presentation at City Hall alongside the mayor. No, the real reason we invited you to our home was to pay tribute to a less dramatic achievement, but one that we think will affect Jake's future life much more. And that is the accomplishment of his goal. He aimed to show us that he was worthy of becoming an official member of the Tiger Flight crew, that our efforts to teach him to fly would not be misspent."

The pilot looked from face to face in the audience. "If you think it's an easy thing to finish what you start, consider how hard you've had to work just to keep your plans on track, how long you've struggled to turn dreams into reality. Now think about this young man who did not quit, who adjusted his plan when he faced adversity, who succeeded against long odds. And remember that he's only twelve years old—just think what he'll do with the rest of his life.

"So, I hereby present to Jake Skyler our official Tiger Flight patch." He lifted from the portfolio the blue shield rimmed with yellow, leaned down, and patted the emblem into place on the Velcro sewn into the right chest of Jake's flight suit. "And, finally, in keeping with more than eighty years of tradition, we have awarded Jake a call sign to commemorate his memorable deed. I'm honored to present to you Tiger Flight's newest crew member: 'Grinder.'"

From the portfolio, Sunny lifted a small black patch and pressed it against the Velcro on Jake's left side, next to his heart. Etched onto the patch was "Tiger Flight Crew" and, above this, his new, official name: Jake "Grinder" Skyler.

Sunny stepped back into line with military precision. All of the pilots honored Jake with a proud, sharp salute. He returned the gesture as the hangar erupted with cheers and wild applause.

Jake turned around to face the crowd, which rose as one and gave him a standing ovation. He savored it for a long moment. Then he looked down at his Tiger Flight patch and his call sign, and set a new goal. He was eager to get started on his plan immediately.

First, though, he stepped from the stage and hugged his mom and dad.

A Note from the Tiger Flight to Our Readers:

Friends, we'll make you the same offer that we made to Jake. If you'll work with your mom, dad, teacher, or other adult to complete the goal list on the following page and send it to us, we'll save a Tiger Flight patch here at our hangar for you, too. When you complete your goal, send the next page to us and we'll mail your patch.

Remember, any goal you set and accomplish can earn you the patch. Make it an important goal—challenge yourself and see what amazing things you can do.

Good luck from Winder, TC, Sunny, Fury, and Bones!

The Tiger Flight might be performing at an air show in your area. We would all like to meet you! For a list of our upcoming appearances, photos and videos of our planes, and more, please visit our website:

www.tigerflightfoundation.org

STEP #1: Set a Goal to Reserve Your *Tiger Flight* Patch!

Fill out and send this form and we'll hold a patch for you at our hangar until you complete your goal.

Your Name: ______________________________

Street Address (or P.O. Box Number): ______________________________

____

City: ______________________________

State: _____ Zip Code: ______________

E-mail (if you have one): ______________________________

Tell us your goal: ______________________________

Describe your plan: ______________________________

____

Tell us the date when you want to reach your goal: ______________

____

To be completed by the parent, guardian, or teacher for verification that goal was set—

Name: ______________________________

Signature: ______________________________

Phone Number: ______________________________

E-mail: ______________________________

Detach this page and make a copy before mailing it to:

TIGER FLIGHT PRESS
1285 Willeo Creek Drive
Roswell, GA 30075

STEP #2: I Achieved My Goal—
Please Send My *Tiger Flight* Patch!

Congratulations!

Fill out and send this form and we'll mail your patch to you.

Your Name: ____

Street Address (or P.O. Box Number): ________________________

____

City: ____

State: _____ Zip Code: ______________

E-mail (if you have one): ________________________________

Restate your goal: ______________________________________

Tell us the date when you achieved your goal: __________________

____

To be completed by the parent, guardian, or teacher for verification that goal was achieved—

Name: ____

Signature: ____

Phone Number: ____

E-mail: ____

Detach this page and make a copy before mailing it, along with a $4 check to cover shipping and handling made payable to the *Tiger Flight Foundation*, to:

TIGER FLIGHT PRESS
1285 Willeo Creek Drive
Roswell, GA 30075

Shortly after we receive this, your ***Tiger Flight*** patch will be winging its way to you!

Printed in the United States
130205LV00004B/1-138/P